MW00377615

SAMMY

A Novel

by
Joel Momberg

Copyright © 2018 by Joel Momberg

Published by Born Young Publishers
P.O. Box 7161
St. Petersburg, FL 33734
www.iwasbornveryyoung.com

ISBN 978-0-578-40788-3

All rights reserved. No part of this publication may be reproduced,stored in
a retrieval system, or transmitted in any form or by any means—electronic,
mechanical, photocopy, recording, or any other—except for brief quotations
in printed reviews, without the prior permission of the author.

To Jodie

Thx.

To Wayne, who left us far too soon ...
irreplaceable as a brother
and even harder to replace as a drummer.

Maybe one night we'll grow wings and we'll fly...
    Stare into space and count stars in the sky.

We might fight dragons and rescue the queen...
    It's the magic of living a dream.

Daddy Don't Turn Out the Light
by Joel Momberg

ACKNOWLEDGEMENTS

Many thanks to all those who have helped me to write *Sammy: A Novel*.

My wife, Debbie who insisted that we buy a condo on Pass a Grille so that we could have a getaway ... leads that list. She has been the most selfless and supportive partner by allowing me to kick her out of the condo and hole up for weeks by myself with my laptop perched in front of the most magnificent view she wasn't allowed to see.

To all those with whom I shared my initial manuscript. I know many of you never read it but you lied to me and told me how great it was just to shut me up and keep writing.

Bill Brand, my good friend, was one who not only read it but was so kind and instructive in his written review.

My kids were too busy to read, but I still love them and they inspired much of the "personal" history that you will see inside.

My parents, Esther and Sam, who were the inspiration for the lead characters. Even though they are no longer with me, they live on through those that know and love them.

My brother Wayne, who passed away more than 20 years ago was the inspiration for "Mikey". He was a helluva drummer.

Finally, a special thanks to Dave Scheiber, the best writer I know, who provided ongoing encouragement throughout the process and offered very helpful comments along the way. He also introduced me to additional professionals who have helped me take the novel to a higher plane, including his sister Susan Spangler, who designed the cover and text of the book with care and attention to my vision of Sammy's world.

FOREWORD

S ammy: *A Novel* is a fictitious story, but like all good fiction it is rooted in fact.

If you're like me, when you're reading a novel you might periodically stop and ask yourself: "Is this true? Did the author really know people like this?" It makes it much more interesting if there is believability behind the make-believability, doesn't it?

Actually, I never believe it when I read the disclaimer: "Any resemblance to actual persons, living or dead, or actual events is purely coincidental." In my case, I know that everyone I meet and every event in my life has affected my stories. For me, the older I get the less there is left in my little brain for new information and I can't afford to waste it, so I reuse the stuff that's up there.

I admit it: "Any resemblance to persons alive or dead is probably because they are interesting and I want to borrow them for few pages."

Sam and Esther Momberg were my parents. As luck would have it, the lead characters in Sammy the Novel are Sammy and Esther Levine. Esther's maiden name was Levin so I took a leap and added an "e". Those of you that have followed my blog, I Was Born Very Young that I have written for the last dozen or so years know a lot about my family and some of the interesting adventures we have had throughout my life.

The idea for the novel came to me one day after Sammy had passed away. I started to think about what his life would have been like if he took a different path. Sammy wasn't unhappy with his life but sometimes talked about things he regretted not doing. We all have those thoughts from time to time. For Sammy, when he talked about taking more chances or leaving things undone ... there was sometimes a sadness that came over him.

As you read the pages of the novel, you will learn about Sammy's early life. It is based in factual accounts (with some flourishes, of course). The rest of the family is truly a mix of fact and fiction. My goal was to give the reader a sense of Sammy's "coming of age" at 86.

Sammy is a story that we can all relate to. There are moments in our life that we want to either relive or do differently. Sammy gets to do some of those for all of us.

The quote that precedes this Foreword are a few lines of the song, *Daddy Don't Turn Out the Light* that I wrote for my oldest daughter Nicole when she was about the same age as her little girl, Grace. Esther and Sam loved that song and because it has always had special meaning, I shared it in the novel with Sammy Levine.

I hope you enjoy the journey... it's "the magic of living a dream."

CONTENTS

DAY ONE

Finish the Plan

Sammy Levine sat outside in a wheelchair at the entrance to the Star of David nursing home. He stared into space with his hand resting on his chin. Slumped in his chair, he looked so skinny and drawn that he appeared to be sucked right into the center of it. At 86, he still had a full head of hair with flecks of black peeking through the gray.

Lola Jefferson, his primary nurse, came outside to check on him. "Mr. Sam, are you sure there is nothing I can get for you?"

Sammy continued to stare blankly into space.

"Mr. Sam? MR. SAM?"

Sammy looked at Lola, "What?"

"Are you sure there's nothing I can get for you?"

"Huh?"

"I said, anything I can get for you?"

"A few what?"

"Lawd, Mr. Sam ... you forgot to adjust your hearing aids again, huh?"

"I wish you would speak slower."

Nurse Lola reached over and put her fingers into Sammy's ear to adjust the volume control on his aids.

"Hey. Get out of there. I'm the only one allowed to do that."

Lola laughed and patted him on his bony shoulder. "Okay … just call if you need me. I'm right inside."

Sammy hated days like this. The sun was shining, birds were chirping and happy people fluttered about spreading joy. He felt like shit and this was just God's way of pissing him off, he thought. It should be dark and cloudy outside. A good thunderstorm would be perfect right about now. It would help justify his feelings. What's wrong with these people anyway? Don't they know that the world is in terrible shape? Not just the starving children in whatever-the-hell far-off country in the world, there are people going through serious shit right here in the good old U.S.A.

He grabbed his shoulder, aching with a throbbing pain. "Just another day in paradise," he told himself. He looked down at his skinny twisted legs and held up his gnarled thin-skinned hands.

"What the hell happened to me?" he questioned in his mind, "I was just 30 the other day. Now I'm sitting in this wheelchair at this God-awful place, eating the same God-awful food and spending time with the same God-awful people. Ten years. It's been ten years to the day that Barry brought us to Florida," he thought. "Esther and I hated the thought of moving here. Got pretty pissed at him for doing it. He took away my car keys, too. I guess he didn't have much choice. And since Katrina was bearing down on New Orleans, we really had to get out of there. But to a nursing home? Really?"

Sammy looked through the front door and saw two old men staring at the walls. They were in their wheelchairs, too. "Look at 'em," he thought. "They are just as hopeless as me.

They are sitting there waiting to die. Hey, wait a minute. That's Bert, I think. Thought he died last week. Maybe it's not Bert. We all look alike, the nurses say."

A big, white SUV pulled up to the driveway in front of Sammy. Barry Levine, Sammy's 58-year-old son, slipped out of the driver's seat. He dreaded these visits. Lately, his interactions with Sammy had been fake and obligatory. Barry wanted a father/son "thing" — whatever that was — but they never had it when he was growing up and now he was just growing old and further removed.

"You said twelve o'clock," Sammy grunted as Barry stepped in front of the wheelchair, lowered his foot rests, reached around to the back of Sammy's belt, pulled him forward and guided him up to his awaiting walker, which stood right next to the chair. The walker had seen better days. Barry got him a new one but Sammy refused to use it, so it was given to his neighbor Basil. The walker had a plastic pouch hanging off the front bar that sagged open so that pretty much everything inside was visible: used Kleenexes, three pairs of Fred Sanford glasses (none worked), scraps of scribbled on paper and things with colors and textures that were guaranteed to make you gag at first sight. The legs were capped in front with two standard issue yellow tennis balls. Make that yellow, tinged with orange and brown.

"I lost my ball," Sammy said.

Barry stood there stunned. "Really? Must have been pretty painful, huh?"

"Got another one from the social worker. See? Now my balls are different colors."

Barry looked at the walker and the two tennis balls. "Oh yeah I see that now.

One is a little less disgusting than the other." Then he added, "And by the way, not that you care but it's actually 12:05. I'm five minutes late."

"A play? What play? I thought we were going to lunch."

Nurse Lola stepped up to the SUV as she walked through the sliding doors to say goodbye. "Mr. Levine ... good to see you. Your daddy has been sitting out here for 30 minutes and refused to go inside. I guess he was just excited about seeing you."

"Lola, you always know the right things to say. It's good to see you too. I'm just gonna take this old bird to get ..." Barry, paused, leaning closer to Sammy's ear, and added, "A BITE TO EAT."

"You boys have fun." Lola said as she turned to go.

"No need to scream," Sammy said as he shuffled to the passenger side of the car. Barry opened the door and eased him in the seat. He folded the walker and threw it in the back. "I heard what you said."

Barry settled behind the wheel as thoughts of homicide filled his mind. Sammy turned to him. "So ... what's this play about?

"We aren't going to see a play today." Barry took a breath. "We're going to lunch at the deli."

"That's what I thought we were gonna do — lunch."

"Figured you heard THAT."

Barry looked over at Sammy as he stared out the window. He was wearing a crumpled white windbreaker with ketchup stains on the sleeve, a striped polo shirt and wool tweed pants that looked about two sizes too big. His shoes were the same ones he wore for at least the last 30 years: bone-colored loafers with velcro straps across the insteps.

Sammy's mind wandered. It won't be long now. He had a plan, a great plan. It was at least two years in the making. All he had was time to plan and this one was a real doozy. Just wait until the Star of David residents find out. Even the catatonic ones might get up and dance.

Barry said, "Dad, it's 90 degrees outside. Aren't you hot with the jacket and wool pants?"

"Lola dressed me." Sammy continued to stare out the window as he spoke. "You know Lola?"

"Yeah. Lola, your nurse, of course. I just had a conversation with her."

"I'll have to introduce you when we get back."

"Sure, that would be great." Maybe he could run the car into one of the many barricades along Gulf Boulevard. No, that wouldn't kill him. Maybe jumping the guard rail on the Bay Bridge and leaping out at the last second. "What's the use?" he thought, "Sammy will live well into his hundreds!"

Barry pulled into the parking lot of Haim's Deli as the lunchtime rush was winding down. He opened the front door after pulling out the walker and lifted Sammy to his feet. Sammy blew his nose and dropped the Kleenex in his pouch. Barry stifled a gag reflex and walked with Sammy through the front door.

As soon as they stepped inside, the unmistakable smells and sounds of the delicatessen settled over Barry's senses and calmed him. He spotted Haim Shear working behind the counter, slicing meat carefully in long strips and placing them in butcher rap. Haim learned the business from his father, Izzy. He carried on the tradition when Izzy passed away 10 years ago and bought the building that bears his name today.

"Sam, you're looking pretty chipper today," Haim yelled across the counter as he spotted the Levines. "Is Barry taking you out on the town today?"

Sammy fumbled with his hearing aids until a light squeal signaled that they were turned up too high. He didn't even flinch. Sammy pointed to the meat counter. "Say, Haim ... Make me a corned beef on rye very lean. Lots of mustard and potato salad."

"Coming right up." Haim deftly picked up the salami and said, "Barry ... what can I get for you?"

"Pastrami for me. The works."

"Oh, Haim," Sammy added. "This is my son, Barry."

"A fine looking boy, Sammy." He winked at Barry and played along even though he had known Barry longer than he had known Sammy. "Sit. Sit. I'll bring it over."

Barry folded the walker, trying to avoid touching that pouch, and helped Sammy into his seat. As he always did when he was ready to eat, Sammy took the napkin sitting in front of him and tucked it into his collar. "Did I tell you that Bertha died?"

"Who died?"

"Bertha. Remember Bertha? She used to sit with me at lunch and dinner. She died. Another one dead. They're dropping like flies. I actually liked Bertha. She had a real asshole for a daughter, though. Never came to see her."

"I remember Bertha. I didn't think you liked her."

"She was a complainer but still a lovely woman. She stopped sitting with me about a year ago. Said something about me to the nurses. I guess I didn't have good table manners. What are you gonna do?"

Sammy pulled out his wallet. It was worn and thin just like him. He took out a small envelope that was folded up inside and handed it to Barry. "Barry, I've been saving this for you."

Haim came up to the table with lunch and set down the plates.

"Okay. Corned beef for Mr. Sam and Pastrami for the boychik. Anything else?"

Sammy grabbed the envelope back again quickly. "No nothing. This is fine."

Sammy shooed Haim away as Barry grabbed his sleeve. "Thanks, Haim. This looks great."

Barry took the envelope from Sammy and started to open it. Sammy reached over and closed it. "No, no not here. Don't open it here."

"Top secret, huh? Is this the formula for Coca Cola?"

"What? What are you talking about Barry? This is very important to me. It's no joke."

"I will guard it with my life. The last note is still in a safe place at the house. I remember the coded words … 'sans-a-belt pants in size 34 and a bar of soap'."

"Always joking. Ha, ha, ha. Well it's not a joke, Barry. It's very important to me so try to do what I ask."

"I'm sorry. I will." Barry slipped the envelope in his pocket. "How's your lunch?"

"Too much fat on the corned beef. This should be lean. Haim must be getting his meat from gentiles. Remember Goldberg's in New Orleans? Now that was great food."

Barry stared at Sammy, shaking his head as he watched him eating with his mouth open, spewing bits of corned beef across the plate.

"You know, Dad, you used the say the same thing 40 years ago. I remember sitting at Goldberg's with Mikey when we were just kids. You would say to us, 'Too much damned fat on this corned beef. I'm not gonna pay Goldberg for kosher meat if he keeps serving this crap.' That was right after you'd tell me not to play with my food and to sit up straight like little Mikey who was eating cheerios with his fingers."

Sammy stopped eating for a second and just looked at Barry, unfortunately with his mouth still opened. "Huh?"

"Nothing."

"Well. I'm ready to go if you are."

Barry grabbed the check and walked to the deli counter.

"Oh, and Barry, tell Haim how delicious the fatty corned beef sandwich was. I loved it."

Haim smiled at Sammy and rung up the check for Barry.

"He LOVED it, Haim."

"God's got a special place for you, Barry."

"That's what I'm afraid of."

Barry's mind drifted back in time as he sat behind the wheel of his SUV, just after dropping off Sammy.

Was it always this bad?

Actually, when Esther was alive it was even worse. Barry remembered the way Sam and Esther would fight like cats and dogs. She was miserable for as long as he could remember, blaming Sammy for her unhappiness. Countless times, Esther talked about all the suitors who knocked down her door. She always said that she should have been rich. She should have been with someone that was more her intellectual equal.

It must have driven him crazy.

Esther's father, who died years before Barry was born, was against the marriage from the start. No one really knew why he was against the marriage, just that he wanted "better" for Esther. He worked at the post office for 50 years. A very demanding and overbearing father, he insisted that Esther follow a strict code of ethics. Even though her grades were perfect in school, it wasn't enough for him. She wasn't allowed to go out with boys until she graduated high school and entered college. As it turned out, Esther graduated high school when she was only 16 years old and was valedictorian.

Esther was accepted to Newcomb College on a full scholarship and thrived there, graduating top in her class at 19. Sammy wasn't the first boy she ever dated in college, but he was the first to ask her to get married. Inexperienced and naïve, she jumped at the chance to move out of her house.

It was at Newcombe that she was also introduced to a new society and embraced by people she never even knew existed. They were wealthy and attractive. They spoke about art and music and culture. These were Jews with money, not the Eastern European Jews that lived in uptown New Orleans. Esther and Sam shared that dubious honor. No, these were Lakefront Jews. They made Sammy seem even more insignificant. He was a poor Jew.

To make matters worse, he didn't want Esther to work. He didn't believe in women working outside of the house. So, his meager income was what they lived on. Esther "became" a stay-at-home, make-believe Lakefront Jew, even though she was destined to live on the other side of town forever. She lunched with the girls, played Mahjong and shopped the rest of the day. Credit cards became her best friends. She couldn't stop herself from buying everything in sight even though Sammy was making a meager living salesman on Frenchman Street.

Jewelry, dresses, purses and shoes were like drugs for her. No matter the cost, Esther charged it. When one card was maxed out, she would just apply for a new one. It didn't happen overnight. It was a gradual thing over many years. It got worse after the children were born.

Barry squirmed in his seat reliving his childhood memories.

Esther didn't like kids very much, definitely didn't like the idea of getting pregnant and surely sex was one of those wifely duties that Sam certainly looked to Esther for (with no doubt lots of instruction). But she did it — at least twice. Barry came first and then Mikey four years later.

About that time, Esther switched her focus temporarily from shopping to managing children and the household. She was obsessed with cleaning. The floors were always covered with runners, the couches and chairs were wrapped in plastic and no one was allowed to wear shoes anywhere inside the house.

The fights and the mania got much worse after the kids were born. Of course, Sammy was just unconscious of the whole scene other than when Esther poured her wrath out on him. There was the day that Esther said, "Sam, you never fixed the bathroom door."

"I tried, Esther, but there were too many screws." Later Esther would find him with a tiny screwdriver, bandaged fingers, screaming at Barry, "Why can't YOU fix this, Barry? You're old enough." Barry was 12 at the time.

He was even worse in emergencies. One night there was a small fire that started in the kitchen of the house on Octavia. It was a shotgun style duplex. Common in the city, these houses were called shotgun style because you literally could shoot a shotgun through the front door and pass through every room of the house. The structure was long and narrow like the lots they were built on. Barry was a baby at the time of the fire and was in the last bedroom in the very back. The kitchen was in the middle of the house. Sam started the fire accidently when he knocked a bottle of cooking oil onto one of the burners. He tried to put it out (you guessed it) with water. The fire spread and Sammy grabbed Esther and ran outside.

"Sam, where's Barry?" Sammy looked around as if he would see him lying on the sidewalk. Esther pushed Sammy aside and ran to the back of the house and scooped him up and safely out.

Barry laughed out loud as he drove. In a sick, twisted way, that story always cracked him up. Maybe because it was because he was a baby at the time and didn't have actual first hand memories.

One he did remember and found no humor in was the day after his 16th birthday, when Esther came into his room saying she was having a heart attack. He was terrified and immediately got on the phone to call Sam. She reached over and pushed the disconnect buttons.

"No, Barry. You KNOW your father doesn't know what to do in emergencies … just take me to my doctor!"

Barry shakily got her in the car. She gave him the address and Barry drove like a bat out of hell to the office. He pulled up and thought she gave him the wrong address. "Mom, this guy is a psychiatrist. Where's the heart doctor?"

Esther told him to wait in the car. He was furious. After a few minutes, he jumped out of the car and stormed inside just as Esther was gushing over the young doctor who led her into his office.

"REALLY?" Barry yelled.

The arguments between Sam and Esther got to be less comical and more hurtful and mean after a while. Barry would disappear into his bedroom and try to tune them out or head to the basement and beat on the old green piano that by then had been given 88 thumbtacks — one for each hammer to mimic the sound of a harpsichord or a tinny honky-tonk. When he got a little older he would just head to The Raven, the neighborhood bar, and pour draft beer down his throat with his buddies. New Orleans, after all, was a great place for 16-year-olds to drink all night without fear of getting arrested.

Mikey would gut it out at home, sitting right in the middle of arguments and trying to make peace. Maybe it was being the younger brother, you know, being liked and trying to be the one to get people to like each other. It made him nuts. Apparently it made him really nuts, according to Esther who took him to the same doctor she went to for her countless neuroses. Poor Mikey would sit in the doctor's office and role play with doll characters for hours.

"Shit," Barry said out loud as a car almost ran into him at a stoplight.

Barry flipped off the driver and squirmed in his seat as he angrily pulled away and as the thoughts of Mikey popped in his head.

In the years that Mikey had to go to therapy, Barry was brutal to his younger brother. He remembered how he laughed at Mikey for playing with dolls in the doctor's office and called him a queer and a little baby. If only he could take all those years back. Kids are so thoughtless when they are that age and have no idea what effect they have on their sibs. By the time he did, it was too late.

Barry opened the front door to his condo and clicked on a light. He was carrying a portfolio of music sheets that he laid on the piano. After straightening the papers, he headed to the kitchen and opened a mostly empty refrigerator. He reached for a bottle of beer and a hunk of cheddar cheese. He cut the cheese then laughed out loud at the thought that he "cut the cheese." This routine was part tradition and part superstition. His first big hit was written after he ate a chunk of cheese and drank a six-pack backstage after a really shitty set with a couple of guys he played with a hundred years ago.

Mikey was his drummer in the early years. Barry was spending all his time — and his own money — trying to really make it as a singer/songwriter. Brother Mikey would sit in after he finished up at Sammy's store. They were really close then — Mikey and Sammy — and Mikey had such empathy for his dad. He felt it was his duty to help out at the store even though it was a dead end for him. Sammy was really not making enough to pay Mikey a decent salary and had been through a couple of bankruptcies and a terrible time at home.

Esther started to spend money that they didn't have and complained every day about how Sammy had ruined her life. Usually during these rants, she'd remind him that he wasn't rich, she never really wanted children, and so on. Mikey stayed through it all, living at home and tried his best to work through it.

Barry didn't stick around long after he finished high school. He went to LSU — paid for it by working afternoons after classes selling clothes and moonlighting as a musician when he could at clubs in Baton Rouge playing everything from Twist and Shout to Whiter Shade of Pale. Took him five-and-a- half years to get a degree in Marketing. By then he had really gotten the music bug and rented a place in the Quarter, put his degree in the closet and hopped around to different clubs playing piano and writing songs.

When Mikey started hanging with the musicians, he crashed on his brother's floor in the living room a couple of days a week. He picked up the drums fairly quickly and was really good.

Barry glanced over at the old picture of the two brothers. He had long, thick hair, porn-star moustache, big glasses and looked stoned. Right next to him sat Mikey, holding drum sticks with his arm draped over his shoulder. They were holding a couple of beers and a big old slab of cheese was sitting right in front of them. That was the last picture Barry had of both of them together.

Mikey died a few years later ... on his 30th birthday.

It was a nasty glioblastoma. He survived three surgeries, a bone marrow transplant and lots of unconventional treatments that he heard about on TV. Doctors initially gave him a couple of months, but he lived for four more years. Mikey moved in with Barry during the later years. Hospice came the year that he drifted into a catatonic state. He still ate food with a lot of help but didn't move and he hadn't spoken

SAMMY

a word during that last year. The week before Mikey passed away, he looked right at Barry, smiled and actually said, "Hey, man, I'm going to Disneyland." Just like that!

The song that Barry wrote that night backstage at that crummy club while eating that hunk of cheese and drinking beer was called It Wasn't Long Ago. Dedicated to his brother, Barry wrote about two boys growing up playing cowboys and Indians. A big brother and a little brother who looked up to him as a hero. As they grew up, they drifted apart but came together when tragedy struck. The younger brother fought valiantly and lived his life to the fullest. Ultimately, he became the hero who earned the respect of the older brother.

Barry moved to Florida right after that.

Staying in New Orleans didn't seem so important any more. Memories were not the greatest. He had an offer from an old college roommate to set up an ad agency in St.Pete — might as well put his old degree to work. He would always play music. To this day, when people ask about Mikey, he says the same thing. "You know, I really miss him. It hurts to lose a brother ... but it REALLY sucks to lose a good drummer."

Barry's cell phone rang. The display read WENDY. "Hi Sweetie."

"Hi Daddy," daughter Wendy answered. "Whatcha doin?"

"Working on some music." Barry grabbed up his charts. "You doing okay?"

"Not really. Did you find out anything?"

"I did. It doesn't pay very much."

"You think I should go for it?"

"Is that what you want to do? I think there's potential there."

"I can't work for Fred one more day. He doesn't respect anything I do for him and I just feel like I go backward every day."

"You didn't answer the question."

"I don't know. I want to get out, but if I'm making less money and starting over ..."

"Well, don't rush into it, honey. Doesn't hurt to talk to Phil. You want me to set something up?"

"Could you? Um ... He won't say anything to Fred, will he?"

"No. I'll talk to him."

"Thanks Daddy."

"Okay, now I've got a favor to ask you. Have you called your grandfather lately?" There was silence on the phone. "I guess that means no."

"I did. I called him last week. He kept calling me "Janet." Plus, he can't hear anything I say."

"It's good you call. Doesn't hurt to visit him now and then, too. He's your only grandfather and he's not gonna be here forever."

"Okay I will." Wendy quickly cut the conversation short when she looked at the time. "Daddy, I'm sorry. I really have to run. Chris is waiting for me. Love you."

"Love you too, honey."

Sammy was bored to death. He sat next to his friend Stan, their wheelchairs locked in place, and watched Dr. Schulman and his family do Jewish dances to an old tape recorder that sounded like Alvin and the Chipmunks.

It probably would sound like that even if his hearing was half decent, Sammy thought.

"Stan, you like this shit?"

Stan just blankly stared ahead.

"Yeah ... me neither. Wanna play poker with the other boys?" Stan didn't move a muscle. He rarely did.

Sammy probably liked this best about Stan. He found someone that had to listen to him and not contradict, complain or even talk. Sammy had complete control. Every so often, Stan would break out in the slightest smile on one side of his face and Sammy knew he was in there.

"Where the hell is Lola?" Sammy craned his neck around. "Probably getting a goddamned cigarette." Sammy unlocked his wheelchair. "I'm getting out of here Stan. I'll catch up with you later."

He put his feet on the floor and shuffled himself and his chair past the residents. "Whatcha doin', Mr. Sam?" Lola said as he passed her.

"I'm going upstairs."

"You want some help?"

"No! Go smoke or something." Sammy grumbled as he pressed the elevator button.

Lola watched him get into the elevator and then reached in her pocket for a cigarette. "I think I will; I might even smoke two, you old fart." She pushed the exit door to the patio.

S ammy knocked on the door marked "Accounting." He had been there so often that Delores Cassidy actually looked forward to his visits.

"Hello, Sam," she said as she unlocked the door.

"Hi, Delores. How are you this evening?" Sammy certainly could pull off a perfect "Eddie Haskell" when he needed to.

"Just fine, thank you. And what can I do for you tonight? Do you need computer help on Ancestry.com?"

Sammy shuffled in. "Actually, I'm getting pretty good at it myself, Delores. I was going to ask if I could maybe do some searches myself tonight, unless that would be an inconvenience."

Delores held out the seat to her desk for him. "Not at all. I can stay for a little while if you'd like." She turned on the computer and typed her password as the screen flickered on. "There."

Sammy started to type info into Google search. "You know," he said. "I realize it's late, Delores, I can come back tomorrow."

"Don't be ridiculous, Sammy. I can stay a few minutes longer."

"You probably haven't even eaten," Sammy said.

"I can wait."

"Hey, I've got an idea. If you want to grab some dinner, I can work here until you come back. Just like we did last week. Remember?"

Delores chuckled. "I do." She looked around as if there were others listening. "I really shouldn't." Delores peeked outside the door. "Oh, what the heck. It's not like you're gonna run away with my stapler."

Sammy faked a hearty laugh. Delores took out her keys. "Okay, I will only be about thirty minutes. Okay?"

"Perfect," said Sammy as she locked him in the office.

As soon as Sammy heard the click he quickly opened the resident files on Delores's computer and scanned all the names. He was smiling broadly. Every week for the last year, he came to the office, learning all about computer searches and data from Delores, who was more than happy to help educate him on modern technology. There it was, a notation referring to the "dead letter file." The last envelope and the one he needed to complete his quest. He opened the bottom right drawer and pulled out the stack of letters addressed to deceased residents, which were in the capable hands of Delores Cassidy for follow-up delivery to the family.

Not tonight, Ira Finkelstein.

Ira's envelope went into Sammy's walker pouch and Sammy happily continued his computer searches without a hitch.

SAMMY

DAY TWO

False Start

Fred Pershing sat at his desk eating a huge egg salad sandwich. Some of its contents were painted across the file that had "Kittinger" scribbled at the top. He grumbled on his hands-free office phone, "No, I don't give a crap about Baylor or any of the other spineless relatives that Kittinger has. Just tell them I'm not available for a meeting." He hit the disconnect button with his elbow.

The door opened and Wendy Levine stepped in. "Mr. Pershing, sorry to bother you ...."

"What the hell, Wendy? I'm eating lunch." The words were filled with egg salad and made Wendy's stomach turn. She had a hard time actually maintaining eye contact.

"I know, but these papers needed to be signed before one o'clock."

"Okay ... okay ... just give them to me."

She handed him the papers she had neatly tabbed for his signatures and he grabbed them with his sausage-shaped fingers. He wiped his hands on a napkin and took the pen out of Wendy's hand. She was over it. This week she was bound and determined to make a move. Her dad had offered to call Phil Campbell at Zemp Advertising. He said something to her at a party a few months ago about an opening and how impressed he was with her when she interned for him. "Why didn't I just wait it out at Zemp when I was there instead of jumping at this position?" she thought to herself.

"Hello? Wendy? Where are you?" Pershing was holding the papers in mid-air waiting for Wendy to come out of her fog.

"Oh, sorry, Mr. Pershing." She rescued the papers right before the egg salad attacked them.

"By the way, I want you to come to the two o'clock client meeting with Smith and Associates."

"Really? Sure I would love that. I'm very familiar with their portfolio and I even put some ideas down that I was going to run through Creative for input."

"That's nice. We'll need a large room, A/V and lots of coffee."

"Would you like me to set it up?"

Pershing slumped back in his chair and gave Wendy a very condescending look. "Why do you think I want you there?"

She nodded her head, closed the door and thought, "TODAY IS NOT SOON ENOUGH."

Barry was in a studio session when his cell phone rang. He looked at the display and said to the band, "Guys ... gotta take this. It's my daughter." He stepped into the hallway.

"Hi honey."

"Dad, did you make the call? Please make the call today."

"Um ... I take it today did not go well at work."

"UNDERSTATEMENT. I hate him. I hate his egg-salad smeared lips and his snarly face."

Barry stifled a laugh at the visual that Wendy presented. "Okay. I'll try to set something up."

"No, just tell him I'm gonna call. I think that would be better than you having to do it all for me. He likes you and I think that would make it easier for me."

"Okay. You know, he likes you too, honey."

"Thanks for doing this ... really."

"I'll call you back. Love you."

"Love you too."

Barry searched his address book for Phil Campbell when Bobby Hagman tapped him on the shoulder. "Hey Barry, the last riff we played before you got on the phone sounded a little weak to me. You want the guys to track it again?"

"Actually, the whole thing sounded weak to me. Tell Nate to make it more up-tempo but pull down the bass a little. I'll check back in a few." Barry headed to his office, still holding his cell phone. He pushed the buttons on his phone with his thumb as he opened his office door with his other hand. He plopped down on his couch and put his feet up on the desk.

"Phil, it's me. Good, yeah, I'm good. You too? That's great. Hey, listen ... remember what I was telling you about Wendy and her boss ... yeah ... that's right ... now she wants to call YOU. That okay? Great. You're the best, my friend. ... What's that? ... Um ... No fuckin' way. You are still payin' me that hundred dollars you've owed me for... let's see ... a year and a half. Go talk to my daughter and GIVE HER A JOB. Thanks."

He looked at his computer screen and saw a message from Wendy with a picture of her attached blowing a kiss with hearts and other emojis spilling out all over her face. Her beautiful little face. All grown up now. "Where the hell did all that time go?" Barry asked himself and thought about the night he finished her song.

"Hey curly, come sit next to me." Barry sat on the piano bench in front of his old beat up Estey piano. It was actually a beautiful piano in its day. He rescued it from Sam's basement and retuned it. Refinishing was next, but not any time soon.

Wendy smiled that toothless grin of a 3-year-old and hopped up on the bench.

"This one's for you." Barry started to sing the first verse of Daddy Don't Turn Off the Light. "Propped up on pillows/ Under the sheets/ She looks up at me and she smiles. Tell me a story Dad./Sing me to sleep/ Stay with me here for a while ..."

"NO." Wendy said as she pushed Barry's hands down on the keys. "No! I play! I sing!"

"Don't you want to hear Daddy play it first and then we can sing it together?"

"No. I can do it." And she did. Not very well, but loud and strong. That was Wendy. Determined to do it her way. Barry finally played the whole song for her when she was about 18.

The bathroom door in Sammy's room was closed.
Barry knew that meant he could be in there from an hour to three days. He knocked on the door and called his name. No answer, of course. Barry knocked harder. "Dad? Just want you to know that I'm here."

"Who's that?'

"Your son, Barry ... your only son. Who else calls you Dad?"

"I can't hear you. I'll be out in a minute."

He always used that 'I can't hear you' routine when he didn't want to give a straight answer or when he said something dumb. Actually, he used it most of the time.

"Do you need the nurse?"

"Yeah ... call that bitch Lola."

"Nice. She wipes your ass and you call her a bitch." Barry stuck his head out in the hallway and smiled at Lola, who was talking on the phone at the nurses station. She knew immediately what he wanted and gave the "ok" sign.

"She's coming, Dad."

Sammy's small room was hard to maneuver. Barry settled in between the bed and the wall on Sammy's favorite easy chair that he rescued from New Orleans. It was worn down, just like Sammy. The pillows were lifeless, the seat support was broken on one side and the legs were scuffed and shaky. Barry bought him another newer chair that he hated. He said it hurt his back. Too much support.

On the wall, pictures of Barry, Mikey and Wendy were randomly placed next to a framed certificate from Bnai Brith that proclaimed he was president of his chapter one year, a picture of Esther and Sam on a cruise, (the standard pose behind a life preserver that read SS Sunfish), a small shelf that held Mardi Gras beads and a wooden toy train (Barry had no idea what that meant). On the side table, there were dozens of pieces of paper that had his scribbles all over them and his cell phone lay there in the middle of used Kleenex, unplugged and apparently useless. Barry had given it to Sammy a year ago. It was the simplest phone on the market to operate. When you forgot how to dial, you pressed zero and an operator would do it for you. Unfortunately, Sammy never charged it.

Above his big fat old TV, in a place of honor next to his bowling trophy, was a sleek polished baby blue urn that held the remains of his wife of 62 years, Esther.

Barry heard Lola cleaning Sammy up as he grumbled to her about something else he wasn't happy about. She just ignored him and told him not to fret about "such things." She wheeled him into the room and patted him on the head. "I'm not some dog, you know?" Sammy bellowed.

"Oh, behave yourself. Look, Barry is here to cheer you up." Lola said as she left the room.

Barry smiled half-heartedly. Sammy shrugged. "What's that doing on my bed?"

"Well, Mr. Excitement, I bought you a couple of shirts and some pajamas and some underwear."

Sammy wheeled over to the bed to look. "They steal my shit here, you know? The schvartzes — gonifs, they are."

"Dad!"

"You don't know. The maids are the worst!"

"That's good. I don't think the staff on the second floor heard you. Wanna try that again?"

Sammy dumped the contents of the shopping bag on his pillow. He opened one of the shirts and smelled it.

Barry had to ask him. "Did you just smell that shirt?"

"Yeah, sometimes Walmart sprays stuff on their shirts."

He must have had his mouth wide open at this point because it made a sound when he closed it. "Not that it matters ... these came from Penney's because that's where you always want me to shop."

"Penney's does it, too." Sammy studied the collars, the sleeves, the material and then held it up. "Don't like it."

"Maybe you should eat a piece of it to be sure."

"No, smartass, I don't need to do that. I don't like these."

"You didn't even look at the rest of them."

"Won't like them either. You just don't know how to shop, Barry. It's okay — your wife is just better at it. Can she pick out stuff for me?"

"Karen? She's my EX wife, remember that?" Barry stuffed the shirts and underwear back in the bag so hard that it ripped.

"No need to get mad, boy. I'll just keep these. They will do fine."

"NOPE. I'm returning them tomorrow." Barry picked them up off the floor and tried to hold the ripped bag together. "You REALLY know how to PISS ME OFF, dad." He looked at Sam, who now had on his giant earphones, as he settled into his 'un-easy chair' and faced the TV. His back was to Barry, totally focused on the Bucs game.

Barry walked around to face Sammy, who looked up and said, "What?" Barry lifted away one earphone from his ear. "Fuck you, dad." He let it go and it slapped back against Sammy's head.

Barry stormed out as Sammy called out to him.

"The colors were nice."

Still frustrated and angry from the nursing home interchange, Barry practically threw the bag that he carried into his condo. It hit the floor of his hall closet as he slammed the door. Sammy knew which buttons to push and did it very well. On days like today, Barry wanted to throw the TV at Sammy's head.

The condo suddenly looked stark and cold. Not much furniture left after the divorce. God, he thought, looks like one of those movie sets from a pathetic divorce movie. All that was missing was a half-eaten pizza on the table, dirty dishes stacked up, clothes strewn everywhere. Nope, clean as a whistle. Just bare.

It would be nice to be able to pick up the phone on days like this to call his mom or his brother or an aunt or uncle or someone in the family who could share his frustration. Someone who would empathize.

But there were none.

Sammy and Barry were the sole survivors of the Levine family. He really wasn't close with the few cousins who remained.

He hesitated, then pulled out his cell phone. "Hey ... it's Barry. I'm headin' over to BJs for a beer. Meet me there if you get a chance. I'd really like to talk to you."

Barry grabbed his keys and jumped in the old Triumph Spitfire that he bought on Craig's List for $5,000, popped down the top, lit a cigar and cruised down Beach Road. In 4.3 minutes he would be sipping on a tall, frosty Bud Lite.

Karen Grayson stared at her cell phone as it buzzed and danced across the kitchen counter next to her chopping board. She let it go to voice mail.

"Who's calling at this hour?" Danny Grayson called out from the living room couch.

"It's Barry."

Danny looked back down at the pile of legal briefs strewn across his lap. "Don't feel like talking?"

"I'm killing carrots at the moment." She waved her knife in the air with one hand and the carrot in the other. "I'll listen to his message in a sec."

The former Karen McClain met Barry Levine 30 years earlier at (interestingly enough) BJ's bar on the beach. Barry's band "Chosen" was playing out on the patio. Barry called it Beach-a-billy Rock. Four Jews and a black guy, all friends and coworkers at New Age Advertising Agency downtown. Barry played keyboard primarily, Mick Greenbaum was on drums (Barry sometimes called him Mikey and Mick kinda liked it. He knew it was a tribute to Barry's brother and his place in the band as drummer). Dave Goldman was lead guitar. On rhythm guitar, harmonica, occasional flute and sax was Pinchus (Pinny) Bernstein and Tony (Token) Jones played bass. They had a pretty good following. Beach residents showed up regularly and college students "discovered" them early. Barry and Dave Goldman wrote most of the music but they also did covers for the crowd when requested.

Karen was a fan.

She didn't know a lot about music. She knew what she liked but couldn't tell you why. The physical attraction to Barry was immediate. He was so different from anyone she knew. Karen was all about making sure her columns added up, meeting deadlines at Williamson and Williamson, church every Sunday, and never being a minute late for a client meeting.

Barry wasn't any of those things.

Karen's friend Lori introduced her to Barry after his first set at the bar. "Really, you're a fan?" Barry asked Karen as he sipped his beer. "I thought we had one of those in the crowd. Which one of our songs is your favorite?"

"Well ..." Karen fumbled. "I liked the one about the train."

"You did?"

"Yes. Something about the train ... um Mystery Train?"

"Oh, good song. That wasn't ours — it's Elvis."

"Well, I also liked your song about the Queen of the Roller Derby."

"Leon Russell."

"Um, let's see. Oh ... the Crying one. That was beautiful. "

"Cry For You? Thanks. That WAS mine."

"Yes. Blue Eyes Crying For You?"

"... in the rain. No, that was Willie Nelson." Barry finished his beer. "It's okay. Don't worry about it. Next set there's bound to be something memorable." As he walked away, he thought, "That maybe I even wrote."

Karen shouted after him. "Say, do you know anything by Donny Osmond?"

Less than a year later they got married.

Barry stared at the TV screen at BJs as he sucked down his beer. He had no idea what he was watching. To him it was just moving pictures without sound.

A familiar voice spoke up a few seats down from him. "Hey, asshole ... where you been hiding?"

"As far away from you as I can, Flip, you old shit. Cheers!" Barry raised his glass to Felipe, who returned the cheers by raising his. He motioned him to slide down.

Flip or Felipe (if his mother was talking to him) wore dirty cut offs, flip-flops and a torn wife beater shirt that read 'My other shirt's clean bro'. "You been playin' anywhere lately?"

"Nope. Just doin' studio stuff. How about you?"

"Had a casino gig for the last three months. Pays the bills, you know? And it paid for the new threads I had to buy." Flip blew his nose in one of the bar napkins. "Sorry to hear about you and Karen, man. That sucks huh?"

From behind Flip, a female voice. "Uh, excuse me. Did you just say I suck?"

"Karen?" Flip stuttered.

"Yep," Barry spoke up. "Now that she's remarried, she only comes to see me if I pay her or buy her beers."

"That reminds me." Karen said. "You owe me for January."

"So cool!" Felipe said as he stood up and plopped a twenty on the bar and called out to the bartender. "Hey Jenny, I'm done! Oh ... and two of whatever they're drinking."

Karen looked up. "Hey you don't have to leave just 'cause I came."

"Nah. I gotta run, beautiful. Things to do, people to bother, you know?"

Barry stood and gave him a bear hug. Karen kissed him on the cheek. Flip sauntered out through the doors.

"Aww, well that was a treat. Seeing Flip, huh?"

"Yeah." There was a momentary uncomfortable silence as Karen and Barry looked at each other. Karen finally broke the silence. "So, what's up? You said you really wanted to talk."

Barry turned his stool to face her. "I did, yes. How's Danny?"

"Well, he's fine, although he's more than a little curious about why I came over here in the middle of the night to see you. And I have to say I am a little curious, too."

Barry shook his head in agreement. He took a long slug of his beer and sat back in his stool. "It's Sammy."

"Oh, thank God, I thought maybe it was a problem with Wendy."

"No, she's fine … well … she hates her job and is stressed out, but you know, nothing a little change of scenery can't help."

"Wait …" Karen straightened up in her seat. "I am so sorry, Barry. That was so shitty of me. Did something happen to Sammy? Is he okay?"

"He's the same old Sam I guess — just a grumpier, nastier version. It's not him so much as, well, him and me. Every time I try to have some kind of normal conversation with him he just shuts it down."

"You've been saying this for as long as I remember."

"I know. I know."

"He's a pain in the ass. We both know and so does everybody else. It's just that he's your pain in the ass. Nothing is gonna change that unfortunately. I know it's easy for me or anyone else to say don't let him bother you or get under your skin because we can do that and we don't have to be there every day to take the continued abuse."

Barry rested his face in his hands. Karen continued, "Could be worse."

"It could?"

"Yeah. Esther could still be alive."

They both looked at each other deadpan, then burst out in laughter. Barry's phone buzzed in his pocket. He pulled it out. "It's the nursing home." Karen moved closer as he answers.

"Hello?"

"This is Celia, floor nurse at Star of David. I was calling for Mr. Barry Levine."

"Yes, this is Barry."

"Hi Mr. Levine. I was calling to let you know that earlier this evening, your dad left the facility …"

"What? He's gone?" Barry asked.

Karen mouthed: "What?"

"No. No. He's here. He was brought back in a taxi. He didn't get very far."

"Is he okay?"

"Yes, he is fine. In fact, he's sitting here next to me."

"Can I speak to him?" The nurse handed the phone to Sammy, who just turned his head and pushed the phone back to her.

"He's a little tired, I think. Maybe call him tomorrow?"

"Okay. I'll just come by in the morning."

"I will tell him."

"Thank you for calling me."

"Certainly. Goodnight, Mr. Levine."

Celia Young, staff nurse on duty, put the phone back in her uniform pocket and reached over to rearrange the blanket that draped Sammy's shoulders. "Your son is going to come by tomorrow to see you."

Sammy sat quietly as she talked. "You gave us quite a scare. Now you have to give us your word that won't happen again. You know it's for your own good. You must sign out and preferably with a family member when you are leaving the facility. Okay then?"

Sammy muttered. "Sure."

In his mind, Sammy thought, "I'm not a fucking 5-year old. Why do you people talk to me like I just wet the bed and didn't know that I should use the toilet." He wished he would have said it out loud to shock Nurse Goody Two Shoes. God, he hated this. He hated the fact that he was so damned short-tempered lately, too. Celia was actually a very nice person. Just clueless. e wished

"Okay then. Call if you need me."

Sitting there in his uneasy chair, Sammy looked small and frail. He reached out and pulled the old knapsack onto his lap. He lifted out the urn that found its way inside. "Next time, Miss Esther. Next time."

A single tear slowly made its way down his sunken cheek as his eyes closed in deep sleep.

DAY THREE

A Glimpse of the Past

"So, what the hell were you thinking, Dad? Huh?" Barry walked back and forth behind Sammy as he sat in the lobby staring straight ahead at the fish tank. He realized at that moment that he was actually worried for Sammy's safety. That meant he cared. Did he? It was a thought that oddly comforted him. He cared that Sammy wasn't injured or lost or dead.

He cared right up to the point that Sammy said, "I was thinking I really don't give a shit about these rules or this place or the food … I really don't give a shit about the food."

"And what about your family? Do you care about us? We don't want to find you dead on some street corner, in some town."

"I don't care about that either."

"About what? Dying alone or about your family?"

Sammy stared at Barry with a flat expression. He was absolutely quiet. It was an expression Barry had never seen. He had seen the blank look, the sarcastic look, the angry look and of course the pathetic look that was well practiced with Esther. But this was different. Barry felt alone in that room. At that moment, he was looking at a dead man. He wanted to shake him or slap him, anything to get him to stop looking at him like that. Flushes of anger rushed to Barry's neck and chest. Barry knew right there and then that it was the beginning of the end.

In a week, Sammy would disappear from Star of David … forever.

S ammy grew up on Rampart Street in New Orleans at a time when post-war white residents were moving out of the city to buy in Gentilly and Jefferson Parrish. The "low-rent" market was attractive to immigrants and those unable to afford more desirable neighborhoods.

Ironically, Rampart Street was not only the place to live in New Orleans if you lived there in the 1800s, it was the only place. The city of New Orleans began as the French Quarter (Vieux Carre) and grew north from Rampart Street into what is now Faubourg Treme, eventually linking up to Bayou St. John, in what is now Mid City.

Originally from Russia, Sammy's dad Wolf Levine brought his wife Fanny, son Ben, who was 5 at the time, and daughter Molly, who was 7, from Poland in 1914. Sammy was born in New Orleans just a few years later in 1921. Wolf was a shoemaker by trade and raised his family above a small shoe repair shop on Rampart.

The story that Sammy used to tell Barry and Mikey was that they were so poor that he wore his sister Molly's clothes to school because they couldn't afford to buy Sammy his own. Barry used to whisper to Mikey, "What about Uncle Benny? He and dad are the same size and Benny was older. I guess Sammy liked women's clothing better?"

They would laugh about that for years.

There were lots of stories back then that Sammy seemed to "remember" differently than did Molly and Ben. Sammy was the youngest and the one who was the most spoiled of the three because he didn't have to work in the shoe shop, he was the first one to go to college (LSU on the GI Bill), and he was the first to buy a car, well at least, borrow the money from Fanny for a car.

The Jewish merchants on Rampart Street were a close-knit group. Many kept their businesses there when they prospered and left the neighborhood for the Uptown lifestyle, and many got rich selling seconds and substandard clothing to the residents.

Ultimately, Sam connected with another Sam — Sam Holtzman — who hired him to sell furniture from his store on Frenchmen Street just a few blocks away. Holtzman's was where Sam got his big break in business (if you call it that). Holtzman gave Sammy his first actual management responsibility. His duties included opening the store, closing it up at night and collecting door to door from folks who were tardy with their monthly payments (prior to credit cards).

When Barry was 10 or 11, Sammy brought him to the store on weekends. For hours, Barry would play with the office equipment like the old Burroughs hand-crank adding machines with about 8 rows of buttons, mimeograph machines and lots of paper and pencils.

Barry loved it.

What he didn't love was when Sammy would take him around to help him with "collections." Barry dreaded those days. The people were not happy to see Sammy, some cursed him and many looked like they would be happy just cutting his throat. Sammy simply sailed through these visits apparently unaware that his and his son's lives were in danger.

Then one day, Sammy came home and told Esther to pack everything up because there was a problem at work. Barry found out later what caused them to move to the first of four subsequent apartments — always, it seemed, to poorer neighborhoods and smaller places.

Sam Holtzman had gone to Miami on vacation, leaving Sammy in charge. He never came back. Holtzman had taken all the assets of the furniture store with him. He cleaned out the bank account and left Sammy holding the bag. A week earlier, he had asked Sammy to sign a document that was presented as his new "contract" with an expanded role and, of course, no salary increase.

If Sammy had read the fine print he would have realized that, in fact, Holtzman had given the whole business to him and by signing, Sammy was responsible for all the losses — and there were many.

Loan payments were six months overdue, much of the inventory was unpaid and the bank was ready to foreclose.

Sammy had to start over.

Barry was only thirteen but started working at a shoe store on Rampart Street selling men's and women's shoes. He had to pitch in to help out the family, sharing his paycheck every two weeks. Mikey never had to work. When he was finally old enough, the family situation was a little better and Barry was heading off to college.

While he worked on Rampart Street, Barry learned numerous ways to screw customers and make extra commission in the process. His boss was a guy named Alan Goldbaum. "So here's what you tell the schvartzes when we don't have their sizes: 'I've got just the thing for you in the stock room.' Then you come back here and use the stretcher (a device that goes into the insole as you screw it open to create a "new size") Then you replace the size number with a sticker and ... voila!"

Barry hated that place. Schvartzes was the uncomplimentary Yiddish name that was used for black customers, sometimes known as "schvartze gonifs" (Black thieves). Barry was told to push polishes that were mostly water based and extra shoehorns for a dollar and sheens that spray on.

All had little stickers with 88 on them that you would stick on to your receipt books and cash them in for bonuses at the end of the month. The younger sales guys would have a field day trying to compete for the most stickers and the biggest lies.

Barry would never forget that experience. Later in life he would always be ashamed that he worked there and for years carried the stigma of being in the same "tribe" as the Jews he worked with.

SAMMY

DAY FOUR

Escape to Destiny

Sammy's face crinkled around the edges as he smiled and looked out the back window of taxi driver Ahmed Kumar's car. The night air felt good. It was fresh and a little cool and gave Sammy a feeling of renewal. This would be his last and greatest adventure. In fact, Sammy didn't feel he ever really had a great adventure. Maybe a few pretty good ones? Not really. Not even close. So this was going to be his last chance for the adventure that he never had.

This was his grand plan.

Sammy knew that he needed money. At Star of David, there was no money that changed hands for anything. In fact, residents were not allowed to even carry money, since many were forgetful and prone to misplacing valuables, there would be no temptations for light-fingered staff members and it just made sense to limit liability. So, he needed a plan to find a different source.

The answer came from his old friend Bertha.

"So Sammy ... did I tell you about my sister Sarah's daughter?" Bertha told him one night at dinner (when she still ate with him).

"Sister?"

"My sister Sarah. I told you about her, Sammy. Lived in Brooklyn, married the butcher and had three selfish kids who tried to bleed her dry. They were the most selfish girls. I swear my poor sister had her hands full. Oy, what a mess even at the funeral."

"Bertha … Bertha … stay on track."

Bertha put her fork down and straightened her dress. She whispered to Sammy — not the best strategy. "So, when Sarah died last year, her daughter Isabel decided to steal her identity."

"Steal her what?"

"IDENTITY … her IDENTITY." Bertha said very loudly. About a third of the diners turned to look at her. The rest were as deaf as Sammy.

"She's dead for God's sake. What identity?"

"That's the point. She died so no one noticed that her identity popped up again on credit cards — on credit cards — can you believe it? Isabel got credit cards in Sarah's name."

"That's crazy. How could she just get credit cards like that?"

"She just applied and used all her mother's information. And she just charged and charged and charged and never paid them off. They kept trying to contact her but guess what?"

"She didn't answer. Because she's dead."

"Right. The only way they found out was when she forgot and signed her own name to one of the charges and left her real phone number with a clerk."

Brilliant, thought Sammy.

It was only a matter of time when three of the residents of Star of David passed away (Ira Finkelstein, Arthur Smolensky and Sandy Weiner). That's when Sammy took advantage of sweet Mrs. Cassidy in Accounting. She showed him how a computer was set up, where the files were, how to search, and on most Sunday afternoons when the office was closed for business, Mrs. Cassidy would let Sammy use hers. She would have the cleaning staff let him in.

Sammy had no problem finding the files that he needed with social security information and other personal data. He sent off three brand new applications and got three approvals and three credit cards in just weeks. They were real people ... just not breathing any more. He'd probably only use one but he might live longer and need more cover, he thought. They were mailed to Star of David and, because they were deceased, wound up in Mrs. Cassidy's bottom right hand drawer.

And, as luck would have it, Ira Finkelstein's driver's license was also in the drawer. Sometimes valuables left in the rooms are forgotten and held for the family to recover. This one would up in the dead letter drawer. Since Ira and Sammy had a vague resemblance, Sammy was counting on security not checking elderly IDs as closely as others.

The rest was easy. Airline reservations, hotel rooms and some new clothes were all done in the last month to reduce the investigation time if there was any suspicion.

"Which airline, Mr. Finkelstein?" Ahmed asked from the front seat. At first Sammy thought Ahmed was talking to someone else on his cell phone, forgetting his new identity. "Mr. Finkelstein?"

Sammy jumped in, "Oh ... yeah." He quickly glanced at his ticket. "That would be Delta."

"You got it." Ahmed smiled. "Big escape?"

Sammy was flustered. "Escape? What makes you say that?"

"That crazy ComicCon is in town this week. Traffic and parking are a nightmare."

Okay you gotta calm down, thought Sammy. "What the hell is a Comie whatever?"

"Comic Con. It's just a big conference for people who dress up like comic book superheroes and come together in one big place. My girlfriend is really into it. Can't say I mind. Man does she look hot in that Wonder Woman costume. You know?"

Ahmed looked in the rearview mirror and saw that Sammy was not listening. Sammy was tired. His adventure hadn't even begun and he was already feeling like he needed a nap — or at least an aspirin for the pain in his shoulder and hip.

When Barry got back from the Nursing Home, Wendy greeted him at the door. "Welcome to the Levine castle, sir."

Barry entered and said, "Hello fair maiden. To what do I owe the pleasure of your company?"

"Well ... you are the lucky winner of the Wendy Free Night of Cleaning and Cooking for Daddy Contest! Come this way ..." Wendy led Barry to the kitchen, where the table was set with fine china and candles and at the center was a pizza box with one giant mushroom, extra cheese and onion pizza.

"Uh oh, I'm in trouble. You must need a REALLY big favor tonight."

Wendy giggled and held out a chair for Barry. "Can't a girl just do a nice thing for her favorite guy?"

"You got the job!"

"Hell yeah!" Wendy jumped up and down and gave Barry a big squeeze around the neck. "Thank you, thank you, thank you. I am so happy, Daddy."

"That's great, honey. When do you start?"

"Whenever I want. I know I don't owe notice or anything to that pig Pershing, but I feel guilty leaving the rest of the office without help so I put in for two weeks. He'll probably tell me to leave sooner."

Before biting into a big piece of pizza that he lifted to his mouth, Barry asked, "So what did my buddy Phil say?"

"I didn't really see him. His HR person hired me." She laughed. "Said Mr. Campbell told me that 'unless I found out you were an axe murderer or you ate your children, I was to hire you immediately.'"

Barry almost spit out his pizza. "Good old Phil. Glad it worked out."

Wendy clicked on the sound system. "And now for your listening enjoyment. Here's a blast from the past — from the wrinkled record racks — it's our favorite lullaby that is guaranteed to put you to sleep. Ladies and gents ... Daddy, Don't Turn Out the Light." Barry's melody filled the dining room.

He smiled. "Wish I still sounded like that."

"You do."

"How do you know? You never let me sing the song. Remember? You always wanted to play and sing it when I was on the piano."

She punched him in the arm. "Duh. I was like 3 or something." Wendy hummed the melody and then came in on the bridge, "Stare into space and count stars in the sky ... we can slay dragons and rescue the queen ... it's the magic of living a dream." She lost it on the last note just enough for Barry to hold his ears. "Stop it."

"Ah. You've got your mother's voice."

Wendy gave him another punch. "And my father's feet."

"We can thank your Grandfather for that. His feet have been passed down from generation to generation." Barry paused and looked down at his plate. Wendy noticed that he looked tired and, for the first time that she had ever noticed ... older. A shudder went through her as she realized he wouldn't be with her forever. Grampy was old but he had been old forever in her mind. But her Dad? He was immortal to her, until this very moment.

"How is Grampy doing?" She asked, knowing it was not good. Her mom had filled her in on the call from the Nursing Home. Wendy thought about all those stories about her Grampy and her Grammy she had heard over the years. Barry had made them funny. He never let on that there were many scars along the way.

"He's just ... Grampy. You know? Or maybe just 'Grumpy?'" Barry managed a grin.

She could tell he didn't want to talk about it. She had learned when to let it lie. "Well, I'm finishing up some laundry. I threw some of your stuff in, too. Is that okay?"

"Sure, honey. That's why I love Sundays. I get to see my favorite girl and get clean underwear on the same day!"

She kissed him on the forehead.

endy left at about nine o'clock. She placed his laundry neatly folded atop the dryer. He kept thinking to himself how lucky he was to have such a thoughtful daughter. When Barry grabbed a stack of clothes to put away he noticed a crumpled folded envelope sitting there as well.

"Sammy's envelope." Barry said aloud as he picked up the envelope. Wendy rescued it from his pocket. He looked at the envelope, turning it over in his hands but didn't open it. He didn't have the strength tonight. Sammy had worked on his last nerve. He had those nights when he just thought he couldn't do it anymore. He just wanted it to be over. There it is, Jewish guilt full force. Waiting for the lightning strike to kill him — not Sammy — Barry. Sure. There are moments when he was really funny. And when he was really not. Telling stupid jokes, some so inappropriate that he wonders if Sammy even got the punch line. Like the one he told to Wendy when she was just 8.

"So, what is green and smells like pork?"

Wendy looked up wide eyed. "I dunno Grampy."

"Kermit's finger."

Really? Really? Barry remembered telling his dad how damned inappropriate that was. "Dad! Do you really think that is a joke that Wendy should hear? That's a horrible joke."

"Aw lighten up, Barry. It's just a Muppet joke. It's the only kids joke I know."

"Kids' joke? A kids' joke?"

"It's Kermit and Miss Piggy. Get it?"

Barry was livid, looking at Sammy standing there grinning that stupid grin that meant he thought he just said something brilliant — or that he thought he was pretty funny.

"I don't get it, Grampy." Wendy said.

Sammy started to explain. "Well you see Kermit put his finger …"

"No!" Barry spoke up. "No, I think Grampy has told enough jokes for today."

"But why does he smell like pork."

"Forget it honey, just forget it."

She didn't forget it.

The next week Barry was called by her teacher who recited the joke perfectly after hearing it from Wendy. She had asked her what it meant when she raised her hand in class.

Barry looked at the envelope one last time. "This is very important stuff Barry!" He heard Sam's voice over and over in his head. Just like the last time, when he gave him an envelope with an ad for sans a belt slacks with his scribbles, "I need this." Or the month before when he gave him a fast-food coupon for a free sandwich at Hardees. Barry reminded him he hated Hardees. "I know. You can probably use it at McDonald's. They won't know the difference."

Barry let out a huge sigh. Yes, too tired to read a new note from Sammy tonight. He touched the envelope to his forehead like Johnny Carson did on the old Tonight Show when he played the Great Carnac … "And the answer is: Kermit's Finger!"

Sammy settled into his seat, struggled with the seat belt and adjusted his knapsack between his feet. Fortunately, the flight attendant didn't see his knapsack or she would have demanded he put it in the overhead compartment. He did not want it to leave his side.

Next to him was a 50ish Hispanic woman wearing a sun dress, numerous plastic bracelets, and carried a bag that could devour his knapsack. She had long frizzy brown hair and sunglasses that covered half her face. Sammy stared at the glasses thinking about Esther. Her sunglasses looked the same except they were covered in rhinestones.

"Good evening," Frizzy said gleefully.

"Hey," Sammy managed to mumble.

"So you're going to New Orleans, too?"

Sammy peered at her over his Fred Sanford's. "I guess so. Unless they drop me over Pensacola."

Frizzy paused, looked confused and then burst out laughing. "Pensacola! Hahaha ... good one!" She leaned in closer. "I am going to see my grandchildren. They are so cute but terrors you know? My daughter begged me to come watch them for a week while she and her esposo take a little trip."

Sammy wanted to say 'I don't give a shit' but it actually came out, "That's nice."

"Are you here by yourself?"

"No ... my wife is with me." Sammy said dryly.

"She is meeting you?"

"No, she is under the seat."

Again, Frizzy halted then laughed even harder. "Hahaha — under the seat! you are such a funny man. I bet you keep her in stiches."

"Not really. I keep her in an urn."

Frizzy was silent. She eyed the knapsack and started to say something but thought better about it as Sammy took off his glasses and leaned back in the seat. He fell into a deep sleep dreaming about past lives.

"So, is your given name Samuel?" Esther searched for something to say as she sat in the booth at Ho Chin's Chinese Restaurant on her first date with Sammy Levine.

"Nope ... just Sam."

"What's your middle name?"

"Don't have one."

This was really like pulling teeth, Esther thought. What was she thinking when she accepted his invitation to have dinner? He's just like the others that Rose Faye fixed her up with ... older, probably much more experienced and probably had money.

She was so wrong.

She had literally bumped into Sammy weeks ago when she and Rose Faye walked out of a club on Magazine as he came in.

"Oh, sorry. I didn't see you," Esther started saying.

"Sammy?" Rose Faye said as she looked at his face. "Sammy Levine?"

Sam looked at her closely. "Hey, is that you, Pinky?"

Esther raised her eyebrows and stifled a laugh. She turned to Rose Faye. "Pinky? Did he call you Pinky?"

"Yeah, it was a high school nickname that the boys called me," Rose Faye said as she blushed.

Esther stared waiting for the rest.

"Ribbons. I wore pink ribbons all the time." Rose Faye turned to Sammy. "So, what's going on with you?"

"Um, not much," Sammy said. "Working at Holtzman's for the summer until I get my teaching certificate."

"Oh, Sammy this is my friend Esther Marks. She is a Newcomb girl, too."

Sammy held out his hand. "Wow. Newcomb, huh? I am impressed."

"Don't be," Esther said. "I just study a lot."

Sammy asked. "Hey, I'm meeting a couple of friends for a drink. Want to join us?"

Rose Faye jumped in. "We can't, doll. Gotta get this one home before she turns into a pumpkin. Maybe another night."

"Sure ... sure. Good to see you and, um, meet you, too."

Esther's social life was pretty boring. She didn't even own a car. The night out with Rose Faye was a rarity. Esther took Psych 1 with Rose Faye and became her "project," her Pygmalion. Esther was really a beautiful girl but did nothing to make herself attractive to men and since she was so much younger than the rest of her classmates, she was shy and mostly unapproachable. Esther was also an uptown girl living at home with her parents, not a Billy Joel Uptown Girl, a poor one on financial aid scholarship. Rose Faye was a Lakefront girl and was born with money.

Sammy swirled his remaining few noodles around his plate looking down trying to think of something interesting to say. She's smart, he thought, and really pretty and probably rich and ... aw shit, this is not gonna end well.

"Want to go for a walk?" She asked suddenly.

"Sure!" Sammy perked right up.

They walked in the Quarter for hours, sat on a bench in Jackson Square and had coffee and doughnuts at Morning Call at midnight. "Oh man ..." Esther said as she looked at the clock. "I'm gonna be in big trouble! I have to get home. Do you mind?"

"Let's go. I would not want to be responsible for handing over a pumpkin to your father."

I am so sorry, Mr. Finkelstein, we are completely filled." said Raul, the front desk manager of the Roosevelt Hotel.

"Nothing?" Sammy asked as he thought to himself how stupid it was that he didn't call for a reservation.

Raul handed him back his card. "I am sorry sir ... I don't have a thing."

"Not a problem my friend. I understand." Sammy hoisted his backpack and headed into the Sazerac Bar. He shuffled into one of the low tables in the corner, folded his trusty old walker with the two different tennis balls and collapsed into the leather chair. He reached down and opened his backpack and pulled out the powder blue urn, placing it gently right next to his oversized bar menu. "Esther, looks like we are not gonna see the inside of one of those Roosevelt Hotel rooms. So let's just have a drink at the Sazerac for now and I'll get us another place to stay."

Caesar, the bartender, was taking this all in from his station listening intently. He came up to the table. "What can I get for you sir?"

"Old Fashioned for me, thx." Sammy winked.

"And for ..." Caesar nodded to the urn. "The lady?"

"Why she will do the Sazerac of course."

"Of course."

Caesar had done this job a long time. He knew better than to ask a lot of questions, especially to an old man talking to an urn and ordering it a drink. He smiled to himself. He figured it out right away. Wife passed away, lonely widower can't part with her and brings her to their favorite place for one last drink.

Close but no cigar.

Caesar stepped behind the elegant bar to mix the cocktails. The Sazerac was one of the oldest and best-known bars in New Orleans. Named for the first ever mixed drink, the Sazerac was visited by the famous and infamous. Governor Huey Long (The Kingfish) would visit regularly as well as countless celebrities who played the hotel's Blue Room, like Louis Armstrong, Ray Charles and Frank Sinatra.

In about four hours it would be packed with patrons but for now it was just Caesar and Sammy ... and Esther.

Caesar stepped up to the table and served Sammy first. "Sir." Then he reached over and placed the Sazerac in front of the urn. "Madam."

"Thank you." Sammy looked at his name tag. "Caesar."

"My pleasure." Caesar continued. The curiosity got the best of him. "If I might be so bold, can I ask her name?"

"Her?"

"Yes."

"Esther."

"Your ... wife?"

"She was."

"I'm sure she was a lovely person."

Sammy took a long sip of his Old Fashioned. "Actually, she was a real bitch."

Caesar was silent.

"It's okay, Caesar. The great thing about being 86 years old is that it frees you up to say all the things that you couldn't when you were 40. Plus, she's dead you know? I can actually get a few words in." Sammy smiled that semi toothless smile where his dentures were missing. "You married?"

"Yes I am."

Sammy motioned him closer. "I'm sure she's a lovely woman."

Caesar looked around as if she might be behind him. "Actually ... she's kind of a bitch."

They both laughed loudly.

"Caesar, let me buy you a drink. This one's on Ira Finkelstein."

Barry was beside himself. He had been on the phone for hours with the police, hospitals and shelters.

How could this happen again and without anyone seeing anything at Star of David? Barry was pacing in his apartment, talking to himself. It had been three days now. Sammy had no money, he had no car, he moved at a snail's pace and he had no friends outside of the nursing home. His relatives were all deceased except for Barry's family.

Was he abducted? Was he murdered, lying somewhere on the streets? He couldn't travel anywhere without money of friends ... could he?

Barry's feelings of dread took a different turn.

Overwhelming guilt filled his thoughts. He had wished for it all to end soon. He was so frustrated with Sam that he WISHED it. Maybe it was all his fault, maybe it was because of him.

He stared at the clock. It was after midnight. Next to the clock was the picture that he took of Sam and Esther at Star of David with Wendy.

That was right after Katrina. His mind drifted back in time.

Barry banged on the door to the house on Melody Drive. "Where the heck are they?" he asked himself. Esther was pretty much bedridden and he knew there was a caregiver/housekeeper here around the clock so it's not like they went on a picnic. And there was a hurricane about to hit in just two days.

Slowly, Sam came to the door eating a sandwich. "Hey Barry, what the heck are you doing here? There's a hurricane coming."

"Duh ... yes, Dad. I came to get you and Mom to safety."

"Ah, we're fine. Just another storm. We been through them before ... not a big deal. If it gets worse we will go to the hotel down the street."

Barry quickly looked around the usually spotless house and saw dirty dishes, newspapers and clothes scattered around the living room. "Where's Juanita?"

"I let her go. Didn't really need her anymore." Barry was stunned.

"What about Mom?" Barry pushed past Sammy and headed to the bedroom.

Sammy was calling after him. "Esther's fine. She agreed about Juanita. Waste of money."

Barry was shocked when he saw Esther. She was thin and drawn and spoke in whispers. She also didn't look like she had been bathed in a few days. "Waste of money? I pay for Juanita and I don't think it's a waste at all. In fact, oh hell, when did you let her go?"

"She still works part time once a week, actually. Should be here in an hour."

"Good, she can help give mom a bath and clean this place up a little." Barry looked at the television to see where Katrina was and knew right there and then that Sam and Esther were getting out of there if he had to drag them.

The phone rang.

Barry leapt up to grab the receiver. "Hello?"

"Mr. Levine?"

"Yes."

"Sorry to call you so late. It's Detective Carver ... St. Pete Police. Sir, I am texting you a picture of an elderly man we just brought in. No identification, confused and matches the description of your father."

"Really? Okay, go ahead." Barry waited a few seconds for the text to pop up. There it was! He opened it ... three shots of ... some random old guy ... NOT Sammy. He sighed, "Not him."

"You sure?"

"Yes. I'm sure," Barry was impatient. "He ISN'T my dad. I think I'd recognize him."

"Right. Sorry to disturb you. We will ..."

"Hey, Detective." Barry took a breath. "I really appreciate your help."

"No problem, sir. I know how worried you must be. Good night."

Sammy clicked on the lights to the room he just rented on Chartres Street. Not much to look at but they took cash, didn't ask questions and didn't need his ID. He looked out the shuttered floor-to-ceiling window that opened to the small balcony that seemed to be held up by a few rusty old bolts.

Down below, he could hear the drunken screams of young kids out for a night of partying. One even yelled from below, "Show me your tits." Sammy thought. "I hope he's not talking to me." Although his tits were a lot bigger than they used to be and, well, he always did love beads.

Speaking of tits, Sammy slung on the strap to his knapsack and headed to the place where they are shown in all their glory, Bourbon Street. He carefully and slowly stepped on the sidewalk. The sidewalk in the French Quarter was hard to navigate, drunk or sober, filled with cracks, uneven concrete slabs and not well lit at night.

But Sammy was determined to go to the place he had never been and always wanted to. Either too scared of Esther or too intimidated by the people inside, he had never ever seen the inside of … a strip club. Well, tonight would be different. In fact, Esther was coming with him.

As he turned the corner he saw the lights of Bourbon Street and the endless row of strip clubs ahead. The older ones still had the barkers outside yelling at the passersby "Come on in … two for one until midnight. That's drinks, of course, not women. But it's four to one in the champagne rooms!"

Sammy stopped at the one he was looking for and looked in. "Welcome to the famous Silk Stockings. Step right in, young man," the barker said.

"How much?"

"Ten dollar cover and two drink minimum." He leaned toward Sammy. "You have an ID on you?"

Sammy fumbled in his pockets, pretending to try to find it.

The barker laughed. "I think we can trust that you are over 21. Just messing with you. So what would you like? Redhead? Blonde? Brunette?"

"I can order?"

The barker laughed. "Yes you can. Over there we have Hope, Mercedes, Blossom, Destiny ..."

"Destiny! Yes. That's who we want." He patted his knapsack.

"She's all yours."

The barker waved to a big-breasted blonde in black lingerie who sauntered up to Sammy. "Hi honey, I'm Destiny." Chomping steadily on a piece of dentine. "You with anyone?"

Sammy looked right at her breasts and then turned away embarrassed.

"Well, you're with me now. Watch your step." She led him into the dark club with purple lights on the walls and a long runway through the center of the club. On the wall was a big picture of Chris Owens, the stripper that spanned decades in New Orleans.

Sammy stopped to stare. "Holy shit. I remember her name from years ago. Is she still alive?"

"Yep. she's still dancin' too. Can you believe it? Just turned 86."

Sam turned his knapsack toward him and lifted the flap. "Esther, you hear that. She is still dancing. I told you to get into show business."

Destiny raised her eyebrows. "Your bag's name is Esther?"

"No, no," Sammy chuckled. "My wife."

"Okay, whatever floats your boat." Destiny pulled out a chair. "Let's sit here, handsome."

Sammy slid in and handed her his walker. Destiny took one look and moved it to the wall, using the tips of her forefinger and thumb trying not to touch it too much. Sammy reached down and took out the blue urn carefully and put it on the table.

"Holy shit," said Destiny. "I bet that's Esther."

Sammy nodded his head. His eyes searched the club. "Say — um — where is it that you do the — you know."

"Do the what?"

"I don't know. Stuff. I always heard stories."

Destiny stifled a laugh. "Have you ever been to a strip club before?"

"Believe it or not at my age ... never."

"Hah. Never would have guessed." She leaned in close and whispered in Sammy's ear. "Say doll, why don't we start with drinks? In fact, I'll get them for us."

"Okay." He thought for a moment. "I think I want an Old Fashioned."

Destiny stood up. "Okay ... and I'll order me a Goose and cranberry." She looked at the urn. "Is she drinking too?"

"She likes Sazeracs."

"Ok ... so an Old Fashioned, a Goose and cranberry for yours truly — and a Sazerac for the little lady."

Sammy reached in his pocket. "Should I give you money?"

"Oh yes, you should. And you will, doll face. When I get back with the waitress."

Destiny disappeared into the crowd. Sammy moved closer to Esther telling her how noisy the place was and apologized for taking her without asking.

At the bar, two skinny, greasy haired dock workers were drinking beer and apparently in competition for how many strippers they could insult while they grabbed their asses. One of them whom the bartender called Zipline turned in Sammy's direction. He eyed Sammy talking to the urn next to him and said to his buddy, "Hey, check out the weird dude over there chattin' it up with that vase."

"It ain't no vase, numb nuts," his buddy said, "that there's an urn, where the ashes go."

"What the fuck?" Zipline stood up straight. "That guy is talking to an URN?" He put down his beer. "Let's go have some fun."

"Leave him be, Zip." Zip's buddy held his arm. "He ain't hurtin' nobody and he's a hundred years old."

Zipline broke free of his grasp. "I'll be right back. Save my beer."

Sammy was just about to put Esther back in his Knapsack when Zipline threw his inked-up slimy hand on top of the urn. "Why, excuse me, sir," he said looking straight into Sammy's eyes. "I happen to work for the State of Louisiana Public Health Department and noticed that you were transporting an urn that perhaps holds the remains of someone close to you?"

Sam kept his hands wrapped around the Urn while Zip's hand was firmly attached to the top. "This happens to be my wife's remains, Mr....?"

"I'll be the one asking the questions." Zip was now crouched right over Sammy's head.

"Questions? What questions?"

"Well, sir, do you know that it is illegal to transport and display this here urn in this here establishment?" Sammy was now sweating profusely and losing his grip on Esther. He also felt his heart beating hard in his chest as he breathed in.

"I'm going to have to confiscate this here urn." He swept it up quickly as Sammy lost his grip. "And I'll need to pour the remains out right here to identify the body."

"No!" Sammy tried to stand but Zip held his neck in his other hand.

Suddenly there was a hand in Zip's hair pulling him backward and a knife blade under his chin. "I don't think so, Zipless." It was Destiny holding fast. "Put him down and put the top back on the urn."

Zip's eyes searched for Destiny. He had a weirdly distorted evil smile on his lips. "Now just hold on, Destiny. I was just playing. Is he your date for tonight?"

Destiny pushed the blade in just enough to cause a small trickle of blood on Zip's neck. "Are you fucking deaf as well as ugly? Let him go and put the urn back together! Now!"

Two huge goons who had black tee shirts with Silk Stockings printed in red lipstick across their massive chests, popped up out of nowhere and grabbed Zipline as he put down the urn.

It was the last image Sammy had after the room spun around and he blacked out cold.

When the images started to clear, Sammy could just make out the face that belonged to the woman who sat in a chair next to ... his bed? He was in a hospital bed? The face of that girl texting on a cell phone, chewing gum. "It's you."

She looked up. "Well, he lives!"

"What happened? I remember that Zip guy trying to strangle me and you ... you saved me with your knife, and then."

"Then you passed out. We all thought you were dead the way you hit the floor." Sammy touched his head and felt the bandages. "But you're okay Ira ... or is it Arthur ... or maybe Sandy?"

Sammy sat up quickly, then grimaced and fell back in his bed. "You took my credit cards?"

"Yes, I did right before the police checked your pockets for identification which you didn't have."

Sammy tried to sit up again. "Where are my pants? I have to get out of here."

Destiny stood next to him holding him down. "Woah Mr. Finkel-Weiner-whatever-stein. You can't walk more than a step an hour when you aren't half loaded with pain meds."

"My pants."

She handed him his pants. "Here they are but don't try to put them on."

He searched his pockets for his cards and ... "My money. It's gone."

"Relax. Yeah, I took it." He looked at her and pointed his finger.

"Really?" Destiny shot back. "You really are gonna point fingers at ME? What is the deal with the cards? Did you take them from those poor slobs?"

"I didn't take them. They're dead."

"You killed them?"

Just then Dr. Fred Trestman walked into Sammy's room and casually remarked. "Who'd you kill?"

Sammy's mouth hung open. "Roaches," Destiny said without hesitation. "He killed a whole slew of 'em at my place."

"Well, that's a valuable service around these parts. Mr.?

"Weiner. Sandy Weiner." Sammy didn't hesitate. Irwin Finkelstein needed to be replaced after last night.

The doctor made a note then reached out to shake his hand. "Mr. Weiner, I'm Dr. Trestman. I treated you when you arrived. So it's good to finally know your name. You know we found no identification on you at all."

"All of it was taken from me," Sammy said, "on Bourbon Street ... by some shvartzes." Sammy was oblivious to the fact that Freddie Trestman was in fact a young black physician.

He peered over his glasses. "I'm sure the police will want to know that." He put his pen in his coat pocket. "Now, Mr. Weiner, about your medical condition." He stopped and looked at Destiny, then back at Sammy. "Would you prefer to discuss this in private?"

Sammy shook his head. "Naw, you can speak in front of Dahlia here."

"Destiny." She said loudly.

"Yeah, Destiny. She's a stripper," Sammy said. Destiny gave Sammy a half-lidded look. "It's a stripper name, I guess. You know?"

Dr. Trestman nodded to Destiny. "Nice to meet you, ma'am."

"You too, handsome." She winked at him.

Trestman looked down at the chart. "First of all, Mr. Weiner, I wanted you to know that I adjusted your hearing aids. I'm surprised you could hear anything at all before. Better?"

"Yeah actually ... thanks, doc."

"Secondly, you had a nasty bout of cardiac arrhythmia. In fact, you temporarily went into atrial fibrillation or afib. Do you have a history of heart problems?"

"Doc, I'm 86 years old. I don't think there's an organ in my body that works right."

"Do you have a regular physician? A cardiologist?"

"Not really."

"There's a procedure that we do here, ablation, which would actually help relieve those bouts and might eliminate them."

"Who does those? You?"

"Yes, I do cardiac ablations."

Trestman looked at him. "No, thanks. With all due respect ... Not you."

"Oh, because I'm a schvartze?"

Destiny giggled.

"No." Sammy grimaced. "Because you look like you're 12 years old. How many 'blations have you done ... two?"

"More than 200. I'm 35 years old by the way."

"And my socks are older than you." Sammy looked up at Trestman and studied his face. "Look, doc. I appreciate what you did for me. I really do. But I have to get out of here. I've got big plans."

Destiny chimed in. "Oh, is it Bingo Night at Denny's?"

Trestman continued, "Mr. Weiner, I can't just discharge you without knowing that you have someone to care for you at home. In fact, we don't even know if you have insurance coverage for your stay here."

"You see?" Sammy perked up. "You have to kick me out. I can't even pay."

"It's not that simple. A hospital social worker should be up to see you in about ..." He looked at his watch. "... thirty minutes or so. She has some questions for you and we will take it a step at a time. In the meantime, just relax, okay?"

Sammy sighed.

As soon as Trestman closed the door. Sammy asked Destiny, "Where's Esther?"

"She's at my place."

"What?"

"I figured she would be safer there with all these carts and nurses banging around."

Sammy rubbed his head. "You shouldn't have taken her and you shouldn't have taken my money and credit cards. Goddammit it. I should have never gone to that strip club."

"Yeah? Well fuck you Ira or Sandy or whoever you are. I'll leave them at the nurses station tomorrow sometime with your cards and what's left of your money after I decide what my share is of saving your ass." Destiny started to leave. "You're welcome."

Sammy sat straight up waving his hands. "Wait! Daisy... Denzel! ... Strippergirl. Don't leave." Destiny stopped at the door looking out the hallway. "I'm sorry. Really."

She turned and took a few steps into the room.

He continued, "You have to help me. Get me out of here. I'll pay you more than the cash I had on me. Please just wheel me out of here before the social worker or police come."

"Destiny." She said to him. "My freakin' name is Destiny. Or you can call me Audrey." He looked at her confused. "It's my real name. Are you gonna tell me yours?"

Sammy hesitated. He looked at the door then back again at Destiny/Audrey. "I'm ... Sam."

By the time they reached the elevator, Sammy realized he was bleeding through the blanket that covered his arms and legs in the wheelchair that Audrey maneuvered. It was coming from the site where she pulled his IV line from his arm.

"Oh great," She said as she looked at the blood on the blanket. "I probably killed you. That's just what I need."

"Relax," he said. "It's just a little blood. I got plenty."

"Oh yeah? You looked at yourself in a mirror lately? Skeletor looks like he's got a tan compared to you."

By the time they reached the first floor, Audrey had managed to soak up the majority of the bleeding with bandages that were in the side compartment of the wheelchair Sammy was in. She hated blood. Ever since she was a little girl and had to take care of her mother.

Before Destiny got Sam settled into the passenger side of her red mustang, she moved her big carry bag of lingerie, G strings, two packs of dentine, extra stage costumes, makeup and a pair of black stripper shoes with 10-inch heels. She grabbed a towel from the back seat and laid it on Sammy's seat before he settled in. Sammy left all his clothes in the room because he insisted they leave quickly, so he only wore the thin hospital gown that opened in the back. Yes, Sam's ass was on display for the rest of the parking lot.

"Sit on this towel." Destiny commanded. "I don't want accidents in my car. Understand?" She buckled him in.

"You think I can't control my bowels or something?"

"Uhh ... yeah! You're like a hundred right?"

"Eighty six, stripper girl. And I am not gonna shit on your seat."

"Okay, good. Just keep your bony knees together and we will be fine."

Destiny flashbacked again to Rosie, her mother. She didn't make it to 86. In fact, she didn't even make it to 56. She thought to herself, 'What would she look like today?' She was so ravaged by her disease in the end that she couldn't remember how she looked before the bad times began. Destiny looked at Sammy and wondered why men and women started to look alike once they hit 80. Ears get longer, noses droop, skin sags, hair falls out, even arms and legs start to look the same. It's like there's only one old body model. Destiny laughed at the thought.

Sammy paid no attention.

Audrey Marie Capparelli (a.k.a Destiny) was born 34 years earlier in Michigan City, Indiana. Her father was gone before she was born, but Rosie told her stories about the strong, handsome contractor who was the stuff legends were made of. In her mind's eye, Bruno was a cross between Rocky Balboa and Bruce Willis. Wealth had escaped him but he was always the guy that you could count on to save the day, the underdog who couldn't get a break in life but never let it get him down. Sure, he left his family, but he still loved them, didn't he? After the construction industry dried up in Michigan City, he left on his own to find work. Maybe his intention all along was to move the family once he got a break. Maybe.

Years later, Bruno Capparelli walked into Gold Club Cabaret in Indianapolis. It was the night that Audrey would finally meet her father. It was the first and last time she would ever see or hear from him again.

"What do you charge for a dance and all those extras, honey?" Bruno asked that night.

"Extras? Ummm … no extras I'm afraid. Lap dances are $15 and private dances are $20." Destiny answered.

"Everybody does extras … little girl."

"Sorry, no extras. You might try another girl." Destiny patted his cheek and started to turn away but Bruno grabbed her wrist.

"That's okay, honey. I want you." He grabbed the cheek of her ass. "I like you."

Destiny reluctantly took Bruno by the hand and led him to the back.

It only took him about 5 minutes to rip off Destiny's G-string. She was younger then but strong and adept at avoiding the groping fingers of drunks like Bruno. When he zipped down his fly she placed one of her stiletto heels within an inch of his crotch as she said, "No sir." Eventually, a bouncer threw him out of the club when he stiffed her for her payment.

Later that night, one of the other strippers told Destiny about Bruno and his history at the club. It didn't take for her long to put things together like his last name, his Michigan City address that the bouncer copied from his driver's license, and a closer look at the faded picture of him when he was much younger that Audrey kept in her locker. She had a sick feeling in her stomach when she realized that Bruno was indeed her father.

Audrey wanted to be mad at Rosie, wanted to be furious for lying about Bruno all those years. But she only felt emptiness and sorrow for the dying woman who lay in front of her on the hospital bed. Rosie's life was a pathetic cycle of alcohol and drugs. Uneducated and on her own, she somehow got herself clean when Audrey was born and Bruno left. Rosie managed to raise Audrey with some semblance of dignity despite the fact that she, too, was a dancer. She was certainly not proud of being a dancer but she never apologized for it, either. Audrey was hired on as the door girl when she was just able to get a job. Money was tight and they needed the extra income at home. Rosie hated to see Audrey working at the club but knew that there were very few options for her.

When Rosie died, Audrey took her place on stage. She tried to do more — saving her money for school and trying the odd office job now and then. But the money she made at the club was too good to turn away from. Some nights she'd walk away with $2000 in tips … some nights she had ten bucks. But most of the time she did well when there was a crowd. She was a beautiful girl and knew how to play the game.

"**H**oly shit! Is this Finkelstein?" The voice came from a skinny redhead sitting on a red velvet couch with a Marlboro menthol sticking out of her lips. Sammy looked at the freckly face with the blank stare. In the background, something was playing that sounded like the same shitty "I'm gonna fuck you up, white boy" music that Sammy just heard in the club. God, he thought, don't you hear enough of that shit at work?

"His name is Sam," Destiny said. Then she turned to Sammy. "This is Sally. She lives in the apartment on the fourth floor. " Sammy nodded his head in her direction. "Sally works at the club with me."

Really? What a shock, Sammy thought to himself. Then out loud he said, "You have a Mustang too?"

Sally looked down her nose and answered with dry sarcasm. "Who me? I'm still paying off my Dodge Charger."

"Just thinking about Mustang Sally, you know?" Sally continued to stare. "Wilson Pickett? Mustang Sally?"

"What's a Wilson Pickett?"

Sammy shook his head. "Another teenager … It's just an old song." He motioned to the sound system. "Not nearly as good a melody as this."

"I know, right?" Sally perked up and smiled that 20-year old empty-headed smile.

Destiny showed Sammy the bedroom and grabbed a pair of leather pants that were hanging on the door. "Here, put these on. Not sure what size they are."

"Ohhh. I remember the guy who used to wear those. Might be long in the crotch, gramps." Said Sally batting her eyes.

"Shut up, Sally."

Sammy stepped through the door and closed it.

Sally took the Marlboro out of her mouth and started to tap the ashes into the container next to her that was now visible to Destiny.

"No, Sally!" Destiny rescued Esther's urn right before Sally deposited the long cigarette ash dangling off the Marlboro. "That's his wife!" She said in a hoarse, loud whisper.

"She ain't complaining, Des."

Destiny scooped it up and closed the lid. "Damn girl. You are thick."

Sammy opened the door to look into the den and spied the urn in Destiny's arms. "Oh, there's Esther," he said. "Just gonna ask where she was."

"Yep." Destiny said. "Just like you left her."

There was a pretty good-sized crowd on BJs patio. Barry's old band, Chosen, was playing for an audience for the first time in 30 years. Actually, it was exactly 30 years ago to the day on that very stage.

Dave Goldman had been planning this reunion for at least six months.

Barry looked out into the crowd. Wendy was right in front with her mom and her stepdad. He had to admit it was really cool that Danny came with Karen. He could have been the typical second husband asshole who stayed away from all the first family stuff. But he didn't and he appreciated what that meant to Wendy. It was good to see all of them together. Even Flip floated around behind them.

Ironically, the stress of the last week trying to find Sammy and worrying if he were alive or dead pulled everyone closer together. They all wanted to help and that comforted Barry. He looked out at the other old familiar beach faces — tan and leathered like always but now there was grey stubble on their chins. And that was just the women! Barry laughed to himself. He might use that line when they started the next set. Or maybe not.

The banner over the stage had a big Jimmy Buffet-looking gator standing erect, with a Star of David glistening out of one of the oversized gator teeth in his mouth. The Gator wore a big gold chained necklace with CHOSEN emblazoned in the middle. The timeless band logo looked a little bit faded but still gave Barry that sense of pride.

On either side of him stood the "four Jews and the black guy." Together again. Token Jones, 40 pounds heavier but still smooth on bass ... Pinny on sax, still wearing the same flowered shirt from the old days ... DG on lead, wearing his baseball cap backward like he always did, except it covered skin and not the long golden locks of the past ... Mick on drums, wife-beater shirt covering a trace of a beer belly but pretty much unchanged. And the ghost of brother Mikey, his first drummer, trailing overhead.

Finishing the last flourish of Fats Domino's Jambalaya, Barry grabbed the mic and spoke to the crowd. "Hey, thank you ... thank you. Wow. 30 years huh?" he said. "I would have never guessed that much time had passed ... until I looked out at the crowd at you old beach bums who are really just as ugly as I remembered." Laughter broke out amid shouts of "look in a mirror!" "speak for yourself!"

"Okay, okay," Barry replied. "Maybe I was a little too harsh." He walked over to DG and lifted his cap. "then again ..." More laughter as DG grabbed his cap and laughed as he plopped it back in place. "Anyway, tonight really is a special night for us. We are so honored that you are spending it with us. Friends and family are truly what it's all ..."

His voice trailed off as it suddenly hit him. His own dad was missing from this picture. His anger with Sammy the man gave way to great sorrow for the loss of Sammy the father. As much as Barry wanted to kill him when he acted like such a jerk, he realized right then and there how much he really loved his dad. He looked at Wendy and Karen. Both were dabbing their eyes. He continued haltingly and finally regained composure. "Sorry about that, folks. Been a helluva week for us. Anyway, it feels so good to be here tonight with you. We are gonna take a break before we do our last set of the night. So drink up! We will be right back. "

A loud burst of cheers and applause filled the air as Barry stepped off stage into the arms of Wendy, who was now crying her eyes out. As Barry held her he whispered to her, "I was going to call you onstage to sing Daddy, Don't Turn Out the Light, but I thought we might not get through it."

"You think?" Wendy half laughed and half cried.

Barry's phone rang. He looked at the display and it showed unknown. "Damned solicitors. I am over it ... now they call cell phones." He answered, "Hey if this is somebody hitting me up for money ..."

"Barry?"

Barry froze. The blood drained from his face. "Dad?" There was silence at first on the other end. "Dad, is that you?" There were looks of shock in all the faces circling Barry.

"Yes son. It's me." Sammy continued "Now Barry ..."

"Where are you? What is going on? Are you okay? Are you hurt?"

"I'm fine ... I'm fine. Listen, I know you've probably been a little worried."

"A little worried? A LITTLE WORRIED?"

Sammy continued. "Barry, there were some things I had to do. I wanted to tell you but I knew you would try to stop me and this is important. I'm going to finish what I started out to do and I'm not sure how long that's going to be."

"What things? Tell me. Tell me now. I'll ... I'll help you. Tell me where you are."

"In good time. If I did now you would want to take me back to the nursing home and I'm not ready."

"Everybody is worried sick about you. How are you getting around? What are you using for money?" Barry stopped for a second. "How the hell are you hearing me so well?"

"A good doctor that I met fixed my hearing aids. My hearing is perfect now." Sammy continued, "I'm calling you from a burner phone so you won't be able to trace this call. I will call you in a few days to let you know my next steps. Take care, Barry." He hung up.

Barry stared at his phone. "He has a burner phone? How the hell does he know what a burner phone is? Is he CSI?" He looked at Wendy. "What is a burner phone?"

As he closed the phone, Sammy folded the paper that he was reading from and looked at Destiny. "I think that went okay, huh?"

Destiny smiled. "Hell yeah. You always read from a script like that?"

"Ahhh, sometimes the memory's not too good and I wanted to get it all down on paper." He gave Destiny his phone. "Hey, the burner phone was really a great idea. I'm not sure what it is but it sounds good."

"All you need to know is that they are untraceable. You can just throw 'em away and buy another one. They are pretty cheap. Strippers use them because we have so many stalkers." She laughed and continued, "and when we get service discontinued because we can't pay our bills."

Sammy tucked in the shirt that Destiny gave him into his tight leather pants. She giggled as he stood there in a silk blouse and leather pants. "So now that you got the pimp thing going on. What's next?" Destiny opened the kitchen drawer and handed him his credit cards and folded bills. He counted them.

Destiny bristled. "It's all there, you grouchy bastard."

"You didn't take any?"

"No, did you think I really would?"

"Well, you know girls like you usually ..."

Destiny turned bright read. "You mean stripper whores like me?"

"No, no. I mean. Oh fuck. Yeah that's what I meant. But you're not ... well, to be fair, you told me in the hospital you would take out what I owed you."

Sally opened the door to the bedroom. "No charge. Forget it. Here, you can sleep in this room tonight if you want. I opened up the sofa bed. Sometimes Sally crashes here when she is too fucked up to make it up the stairs."

Sammy leaned on his walker. "Desti ... um, Audrey ... I really thank you for saving my ass. Let me give you some money."

"Oh now you're Mr. Generous?" Sammy tried to give her a ten dollar bill. She looked at it wide eyed. "Wow! What did I do to deserve this?"

"Too much?"

Destiny just laughed. "You're too much, Mr. Finkelwiener!" She patted his face. "For an asshole, you're actually very sweet. Good night."

She closed the door.

SAMMY

DAY FIVE

Something's Fishy

Sammy sat in the easy chair next to the sofa bed. He looked around the room. Next to him was a white desk with a wooden chair painted with little daisies all around.

On the desk, Sammy noticed lots of pictures in an assortment of frames. One had a picture of a younger Audrey in a ballet tutu, pink sweatshirt and tennis shoes. She had a wide toothless grin and was bowing to the camera. Another frame held a picture of a very attractive woman with lots of makeup kissing a baby. Must be her mom, Sammy thought. Scattered next to the pictures were hairbrushes and a hairdryer and a Styrofoam head with a blonde wig. The mirror had more pictures taped to the sides. Looked like faces of girls at the club — most of them were either coming out of their tops or were sticking out their butts.

The walls were painted pink. There was a colorful poster with the saying: "Change your thoughts and you change your world" and a black poster with a small box checked and large white letters screaming: "GET SHIT DONE!"

Racks and coat hooks were randomly placed around the room with a variety of shawls, robes, beaded necklaces and a wind chime. One nearly dead palm was stuck in a corner as well.

The sofa bed was draped with two crocheted covers. There was a kind of organized chaos going on in that room.

Sammy started to take off his shoes but felt tired. He leaned back in the chair and closed his eyes.

A loud crash in the next room woke Sammy from a sound sleep. He sat up straight in his chair and felt a searing pain from his neck down the entire right side of his back. "Shit!" He said out loud. He looked at the clock on the side table ... it was 9:05 AM. Esther's urn was next to the clock and on the sofa bed was a shopping bag.

He slowly got up and gingerly stretched out the kinks. Opening the bag he pulled out slacks and shirts and underwear. e He He turned to Esther's urn. "Little E, looks like our new friend Audrey did some shopping for me. You like these better than the leather number? Yeah, me too."

Sammy opened the door and saw Audrey sweeping up a broken dish.

"Sorry. I didn't mean to make so much noise out here. You were sleeping pretty hard there, Sammy." Audrey said. She spotted the pants in his hand. "I see you found the stuff I picked up at Walmart."

"Yeah, it was nice of you to get me these new duds here." He took out his cash. "So Audrey, what do I owe you for the clothes?"

Audrey held up her hand. "Already taken care of."

"But I want to pay for them."

"You did. Took it from you this morning." She started to straighten and fold his clothes.

"So I've gotta get to work and, well, I can drop you somewhere. I know a hotel that's pretty reasonable down the block. Unless you want to just look for something else."

Sammy put a hand on hers and asked her to sit next to him. "You think I can stay here just a little longer?"

She stood up quickly. "Listen, I don't mind trading insults with you for a day or two but I gotta go to work and have my life back you know?"

"You have been a godsend. I mean it." Sammy said as he nodded and winked at Esther's urn.

"Don't do that. It freaks me out when you do that."

Sammy laughed. "Sorry, force of habit." He patted the couch for her to sit. "I can pay you. I WILL pay you whatever you want to help me get through the next week. Can you do a week?"

Destiny was silent and looked at Sammy's face. She never really had a father. This was the closest thing she had to a male who she could trust and he was kind of like an old grouchy grandfather. Was it really a week?

"So," she asked, "What if this 'thing' you have to do takes longer than a week?"

"It won't. It can't. I'll explain later. If it does than I have to cut it short. But that's okay too."

"But you told your son you didn't know how long ..."

"I know. It was because I don't want him to know everything. I have my reasons."

Audrey wrinkled her nose. "All right. I know I'm going to regret this. But it's gonna cost you." Sammy started to speak but she interrupted: "More than ten bucks!"

As the red mustang came to a stop, Audrey pulled out the little piece of paper that Sammy had given her at the apartment. "Is this the address?" She asked.

"That's the address that Captain Tony gave me over the phone." Sammy said.

"Who the hell is Captain Tony?"

"He's the guy with the boat. Don't worry about it. You'll see when we get there."

Audrey sighed. "You know it would be nice if you could like tell the whole story at one time instead of, well, telling me about Captain Tony and a boat and writing stuff like this. You've got really shitty handwriting by the way. There is no such street as Careview Drive."

"That's Clearview Drive. Maybe you should put on your glasses."

"Whatever."

They pulled up to Captain Tony's place at the Lakefront at noon. It wasn't much of a place, just a shack on a pier with a 32-foot Bayliner tied up next to it. Sammy and Audrey stepped inside to a small desk and a bearded crusty old guy smoking a cigar who looked older than Sammy.

"You Tony?" asked Sammy.

"Nope," the crusty guy said as he continued to smoke his cigar and look into Sammy eyes. There was a long silence as both of them stared each other in the eyes.

"Don't I know you?" asked Sammy.

"Nope."

"You're Dickie Broussard, right?"

Crusty guy studied Sammy for a minute.

"Who wants to know?"

"Sammy. Sammy Levine." Sammy said.

"Holy crap. Sammy? You look like shit man. Is that really you?" He was standing now right across from Sammy.

"Really? I look like shit? Have you looked in a mirror?"

Audrey mumbled. "Have you both looked in a mirror in the last century?"

Dickie gave Sammy a big bear hug and lifted him right off the floor. Sammy stayed frozen with his arms to his sides. Captain Tony walked in just as the love fest died down. Tony was a younger version of Dickie. No cigar and about two inches taller but clearly a chip off the old block. Dickie said to Tony, "Son. This here is Sammy Levine or Lumpy Levine as we used to call him."

"Lumpy?" said Audrey with a grin.

"Nice to meet you, Lumpy." Tony held out a hand.

"Sammy will do fine." Sammy said. "Hey I called about a half day fishing trip this afternoon. Still on?"

"You did? Hmmmm, all I had was a reservation for someone named Wiener." Tony looked up and laughed. "Unless you are Lumpy Wiener!"

They all roared at the joke.

"Actually," he lowered his voice, "This is Sandy Wiener." He gestured to Audrey.

Dickie looked her over and then leaned in and said. "Lumpy Wiener?" He burst out laughing. Audrey was not happy. She leaned in nose to nose. "Fat Asshole?"

After a pregnant pause, all four of them burst out laughing.

"Okay, well, let's get down to business. We need to get you on the water." Tony said. "Now half day will cost you $55 plus taxes and a service charge to clean the fish if you'd like."

Sammy pulled out cash.

"You can do that later Mr. Levine as long as you agree to the cost and you fill out some papers for liability. Here." He pointed to a signature line. "Have you ever fished before?"

"Um, no; this is the first time for the wife and I," Sammy said.

"You two are husband and wife?" Dickie asked.

"Oh no," Sammy jumped in. "She's a stripper."

Audrey looked down her nose at him.

Dickie and Tony shared a glance. "Okay then. Well what do you say we get aboard?"

"I am just going to make a quick call and meet you on board," Sammy said.

It was truly a beautiful afternoon. Not too hot and there was even an unusually refreshing Louisiana breeze. Even Audrey had to admit it. As much of a pain in the ass as Sammy could be and with all the crap she had to deal with at work and home when she finished his "adventures," she was actually having a good time. She had to let that thought sink in. "Having a good time." Seemed like years since she could say that.

"What do you think?" Sam asked as he held his rod across the stern. Audrey sat next to him and peered over her bright yellow-rimmed sunglasses.

"It doesn't suck." She answered. She watched as he reeled in his line, checked his bait and cast out over the hull to her right. Captain Tony was at the controls on the bridge. His dad Dickie didn't make the trip. He was minding the store on the pier.

"So, you never fished before, huh?" Audrey asked as she watched his hook hit the water.

"Oh yeah. Plenty of times."

"I thought you said ..."

"I know what I said." He cocked back his big-rimmed hat. "I lied. Not about Esther. She hated fishing. She never did it and never wanted to."

Audrey walked over to him. "So why are we here? And why is this the first stop of your big adventure?"

"Oh no. First stop was the strip club. First time for me! And first time for Little E." He moved Audrey's rod to the left. "Careful. You are pretty close to the motor."

"So, this is the second stop?"

"That's right." He looked to his right to make sure Captain Tony wasn't within earshot. "Dickie Broussard is number 2."

"I need a beer for this." Audrey said as she put her rod in the holder, lifted the lid on the large ice chest behind them and grabbed two Buds. She popped them both open and handed one to Sammy.

"Cheers!" Sammy toasted and settled in. He put his rod in the holder as well. "Dickie Broussard is not a nice man. In fact the Dickie that I knew in high school was really a dick. He was my daily tormentor, the bully who stole my lunch money, slashed my bike tires and more than once broke my nose. You know the nickname he gave me? Lumpy?" Audrey stifled a laugh. "Well, it was because by face and my head were all lumpy by the time he got finished."

Audrey touched his arm. "I'm sorry, Sammy." Audrey and Sammy took long gulps. "You'd think he was your long, lost friend the way he hugged you in there."

"I know. I guess time has a way of helping you forget what an asshole you were," he continued as he looked at Tony. "There was another kid who went to high school with us, named Philip Sizeler. He had a long, hooked nose and was about half my size. Everybody called him The Mole. He actually liked it and signed his name that way sometimes. Well, Dickie loved picking on Philip even more than me. I remember a day when we were riding our bikes and in swoops Dickie from a side street, cutting us off in an alley. He asked us how much money we had on us, just like always. Philip took out a dollar and handed it to him. When I reached into my pocket, it was empty. I walked toward him and he looked at my empty hand and punched me so hard in the face that I saw stars and fell over my bike. Philip got angry and that little skinny guy ran his head right into Dickie's balls. Oh, man, was he pissed. Dickie swore to get Philip the next day." Sammy looked out at the water. "The next day, the janitor found Philip unconscious next to a bathroom sink bleeding from his ears. Philip never came back to school and we never knew what happened to him. I knew after that, I would get even with that asshole. Somehow."

"Wait, I'm confused." Audrey said. "So you came here to fish on his boat, let him hug you and pay him money. I don't get it." Audrey's rod bent slightly up and down.

"I have this lawyer friend in Miami who checked up on Mr. Richard Broussard. It seems that our friend Dickie has been on the radar with the Feds for a couple of years for drug trafficking. They couldn't pin anything on him until just last month."

Audrey's reel was now dancing up and down but unnoticed as she was enthralled with the story.

"The attorney that I know has a client who knows Mr. Broussard. In fact, they did a little business together. My attorney friend approached his client who was facing a 20-year sentence in the federal penitentiary. So guess what? They worked out a deal with the prosecutor for an abbreviated sentence in exchange for?" Sammy looked at Audrey.

"Information about the Dick!"

"Bingo. And I was to call the number he gave me when I actually came in contact with Dickie."

Excited, Audrey said. "Which you did when you stepped outside!"

Tony turned and saw Audrey's rod bend over in half. "Hey," he yelled. "You hooked a big one!"

They both said in unison, "Yes, we did."

"Wendy. What do you think about this top?" Karen called out to her daughter as she held up her latest find from the center rack at Nordstrom. They had just had lunch at the new seafood place on the second floor of the mall and were shopping for some work outfits for Wendy's new job.

"That one's cute. I just don't like the yellow too much."

"Yeah. Me either. Maybe if they have one that's more muted."

Wendy pulled out a striped poplin blouse from the other side of the rack. "I like this one."

Karen shifted to the other side and looked at the label. "Hmmm. Ann Taylor. Very nice. Try it on." She stepped into the fitting room and slipped it on. Karen followed her in with three more tops.

"Mom. I'm a little worried about Grampy. I know Dad is too, but he's been really quiet about it the last few days since he's called."

"Your dad said he actually sounded pretty good on the phone but he's got pretty serious health issues and needs a lot of care." Karen said, "But you know Grampy. He's pretty ornery. I don't think he's quite ready to quit. On anything! You know there's still the spirit keeping him going." Karen grabbed another outfit for Wendy as she slipped off the other one.

"I think Grampy drives him nuts sometimes. Grampy can be a little mean to Dad, you know?" Wendy said as she looked in the mirror again.

"Dad has these confusing issues with Grampy. He's struggled with them for a long time and this latest thing has him pretty messed up. He loves your grandfather but never felt he got the same love and respect in return."

Wendy slipped it on. "This one makes me look fat." She placed it on the hook and tried one more. "You know, YOU never told me why you and dad split up."

"I guess you were so young when we did and when you got older it never came up." Karen smiled "Until now."

"So?"

Karen gathered up the remaining tops. "Nothing to tell really.

"Mom!"

"Well," Karen started, "It just happened, I guess, over time. We were different people, your dad and I. He was the free spirit, creative, sensitive, 'not knowing what he wants to be when he grows up' kinda guy. And I was – boring," she said with a loud laugh at the end. "I was an accountant. All my numbers added up, I planned, I wanted answers and needed data. He actually needed me for that in the beginning and I needed his Peter Pan-ish spirit to lift me at times. Then we had you."

Wendy smiled. "Which one am I?"

"Oh, you are so your father's daughter, So full of life and so creative." She took Wendy's hand. "We love that about you."

"So what happened?"

"I don't really know. We started to get bothered by the same stuff we were so drawn to in the beginning. Dad was kinda finding himself. He was playing music at night but wasn't sure if music was his thing, you know, as far as going at it full time and was afraid it wouldn't pay the bills. Plus, it had him out all hours of the night. He loved the agency but frankly missed hanging with the guys." Karen sat down on the fitting room bench. "My organizational habits were cramping his style and his freewheeling style had me wondering where he was half the time. I'm sure I had less patience for him while he was finding his way. So we just did different things and had different lives. We didn't really spend much quality time together. We just drifted, I guess."

"That was it?"

"Sounds stupid huh? I could get into Freudian analysis of Barry's messed up family life, his wacko mother, his brother's death. He could analyze my neurotic cleanliness and questioning. But at the end of the day, it wasn't working and we were living separate lives."

"It's so —" Wendy shed a small tear — "sad." She sat next to her mother and put her head on Karen's shoulder.

"It was. For a while it was. But we have come out of it stronger and still respecting and loving one another because we share something that eclipses it all." Karen held Wendy so tight that she almost couldn't breathe. "We share our love for you, sweet girl."

S itting in the corner of the stripper's dressing room at Silk Stocking was not Sammy's idea of a great time, but there he was waiting for Destiny to come get him. The girls were loud, brash and seemed like they were always pissed off at somebody or something. There was lots of drama back there.

Of course, he got to see lots of naked breasts and naked bottoms and even naked vaginas. What was that all about, he thought? Girls apparently shaved it all off these days. Looked weird. And that tape on their nipples. Guess it was the law that they can't show the nipples. Stupid law. They really take everything else off so what the heck is that about?

Two black strippers on Sammy's right started to scream at each other and slam their locker door.

"Bitch, you took eight dollars from me," screamed the one with silver stilettoes. "Took it right outta my locker."

"That's bullshit, skank. How I got into yo' locker?" answered the other, standing toe to toe without her pants on.

"Uhhh cause I GAVE you my combination last week when I axed yo to get my panties."

"You just crazy, bitch."

Silver stilettoes grabbed her by the throat and pushed her into the locker. "Girl, I'm gonna fuck you up if you don't give me my money right now."

No pants reached into her garter and pulled out a folded stack of bills as Stilettoes released her grip. "Here!"

She counted out four twenties. "Take it. But I ain't never stole it from you. I just don't want no trouble."

Sammy watched as they both separated, still flinging insults at each other. "She is one scary woman," Sammy said to one of the dancers who was putting pasties on across from him.

"Layla? You should see her when she's drunk. She's just mad that her man took her car and her couch last night."

Looking around, Sammy didn't know whether he was safer in the dressing room or at the bar, Destiny wanted him to wait in the dressing room because Zipline and his gang of misfits were playing pool and she didn't want him to get hassled.

This was much more interesting.

"Having fun?" Destiny shouted to him as she came into the dressing room.

Pasties answered for him. "Oh, I'd say we are keeping him entertained, right sweetie?"

Sammy nodded and smiled.

Destiny undressed and pulled on a pair of jeans. She sat next to Sammy. "So, I told you that the asshole Zipline is here tonight," she said, fastening her jeans. "Get this. He comes over and asks me if I'd give him a discounted dance. He thinks because I almost cut his throat, I owe him. Can you believe that?"

Sammy smiled. "So what did you say?"

"I gave him a dollar and told him to beat it." She gave the outward fist pump. Sammy laughed so hard he started coughing and turning red. "Easy there, big fella. You're not 80 anymore."

He took out his handkerchief and wiped his forehead. "Woo, you are quite the catch, Audrey."

"Yeah. That's what they all say." She opened her purse to count her tips. "Oh, to top it all off, my favorite weirdo customer comes in tonight right as this guy buys me a drink. He stands over my shoulder and just stares at me. Just stares! Doesn't talk doesn't have a drink. Just stands there and stares."

She closed her purse. "So I say to him, 'Homer, you gonna catch flies in that mouth. Close it. And go stand in the corner.'"

"Homer? You call him Homer?"

"That's really his name. Figures huh?" Audrey put on her sandals. "So Homer actually goes to the corner of the bar and stands there. The rest of the night! The guy I'm sitting with tips me and leaves. I work the bar looking for any signs of life. Nothing. There's this bachelor party that came in but Sally and Mercedes got there first. They made all kinds of money tonight doing bachelor games with the groom-to-be. Get him up on stage and their friends throw dollars at you to embarrass him. Take his shirt off. Pull down his pants and have him hop up and down in his tightie whities." She closes her locker. "Me? I got Homer and one tip."

Audrey sat back down. "I have got to get a new career. I made $30 tonight." Sam's chin was resting on his chest as a quiet snoring sound pursed his lips. Destiny looked at him.

His hands were resting on the walker, his back was against one of the lockers and he was sound asleep.

Destiny leaned next to his ear. "This is just great, Sammy. Capped off my evening. No money, no men and boring as shit. Wake up. Let's get out of here."

"Huh?" Sammy winced and half opened his eyes. "Ready to go?" Sammy said, "I am taking you out for dinner."

Pulling on a black tank top, Destiny answered, "Oh yeah? That sounds like a date. Wait. Is this number three?"

"Yes. This is the third stop on the list."

"Where are we going?"

"To this address on Frenchmen Street." Sammy showed Destiny a little piece of paper with a scribbled number. "I think it's a Jazz Club called The Corner Bar."

"I heard of that. You like jazz?"

"Hate it."

"Oh," Destiny said, looking at the urn, "Esther likes it, huh?"

"She hates it too."

"Well now it's clear as mud, Sammy boy. Can't wait to hear this one." Destiny stood up and helped Sammy to his walker, playfully calling out, "Race you to the car."

The place was slammed. Corner Bar was a big hangout for locals and a magnet for visitors who were hungry to grab a piece of New Orleans history and listen to jazz at its finest. Some of the top musicians played there in the past and there were pictures of them tacked up on every wall.

Audrey sat across from Sammy looking at his furrowed brow. He was not happy being here. She could tell this was not his thing. There were wall-to-wall people. It was noisy and standing room only. Luckily, they got one of the last tables. Audrey sipped her cosmo as she cut into her filet. Sammy just had a piece of grilled chicken and a glass of water.

His stomach was acting up again and the noise was giving him a massive headache.

"You hate this, don't you?" Audrey had to almost scream to Sammy to be heard and he was only about two feet away on the other side of the table.

Sammy shrugged his shoulders. "Not my favorite kinda place."

"So. Why are we here?"

He looked across the crowd and after a few seconds pointed toward the corner bar. "Look over there."

"The bartender? Yeah he's kinda hot. "

Sammy gave her a frustrated look. "Not the bartender. The windows. You see those windows?"

"Can't miss 'em. They have to be eight feet tall. We're here for the windows?" Sammy adjusted his chair so that he was only a few inches from Audrey's ear. "Those windows are the original ones for this building. I remember those windows when they were installed." Sammy scanned the other side of the room. "See those light fixtures? They were original, too. You don't see those anymore." Audrey eyed the art deco designs straight from the '20s. The chunky frosted glass stacked pattern held up by a brass base.

Audrey waited for the rest.

"This was my old store. Well, it was part of my old store. The buildings on either side made up the rest of it. Holtzman's Furniture Store. It was here." He looked down at Esther's urn. "Remember Esther?"

Audrey looked down too. "Does she remember?"

"Yes, she remembers smart ass."

A stocky redhead wearing a white shirt, black tie and black pants under a long black apron came op to the table. "So how we doin?"

"Food's great." Audrey answered.

"Glad you're enjoying it. And for you sir?"

"It sucks. Chicken's cold."

Redhead leaned over to look. "Can I heat it up for you or get you something else?"

"Nah. I'm not that hungry anyway." Sammy waved her away. The waitress again apologized and left.

"You are a real charmer, you know?"

"Need to tell them when the food is no good. We are paying good money and they need to know."

"Give her a big tip."

"What? No way. The food sucked."

"She didn't cook it. She served it and she probably doesn't make shit here. AND she's got to be nice and listen to assholes like you all day."

"I don't think ..."

"Just pay it or I'll cut your fuckin' throat." Audrey grinned and tapped her pocket where she kept her knife.

"Okay, okay." He continued his story: "So I was sayin', this used to be a furniture store. My store. It was my whole life when was just starting out. Worked my ass off here. Esther and I were starting a family."

Audrey looked at the urn. "How many kids?"

"Two. Two boys. Barry and Michael."

"Good names." Audrey continued. "They live close to you now?"

"Barry does. Mikey passed away."

"Oh shit." Audrey said. "Sorry."

"I brought the kids here sometimes to visit the store and even help out. They were good kids. Are good kids, I mean. Well, you know what I mean."

Audrey asked one more question. "I bet Esther was a good mother, huh?"

"As good as any I suppose." Sammy stopped. "I mean, it wasn't natural for her like it is for a lot of women. She never really planned on kids. Didn't really like them too much. I think she did it because all our friends were doing it and she just thought it was something she should do. But she tried hard. She had a few issues."

He patted the urn again.

"Issues. We all got 'em," Audrey said.

Sammy took a longer pause as he sipped his water. He looked at the urn and took a deep breath. "One day there was this girl who showed up at the store looking for work. She was just a kid, a skinny little thing with big blue eyes and looking like she hadn't eaten in weeks. She begged me for a job. Said she had been looking everywhere. She was desperate. Tried dancing for a while. Anything to get some money. I told her I'd take a chance on her and hired her to help out in the store with inventory and shipping. She was good. She learned fast. Always wanting to know more about the business. She worked like a demon."

Musicians started to step up to the small stage and tune up their instruments one by one.

"One night we both worked late in the stockroom. It was just the two of us and I remember as clear as if it was yesterday. She brushed up against me when she reached for a box of hardware. The feeling that I had was so strong that it literally took my breath away."

Sammy looked at Esther's urn, still sitting in the center of the table. "Esther. I never told you about this. I wanted to many times but couldn't figure out how to do it. I fell for her, I fell hard." Audrey put an arm around his shoulders as he started quietly weeping.

"I'm so sorry, Esther. I was a coward for not telling you. I was weak."

"Hey. Sammy. It's all right. We all make mistakes. I'm sure Esther forgives you."

He was inconsolable. Sammy sobbed and just kept shaking his head, reliving the best and the worst times in his life as if they were happening all over again. "You know, it really didn't last long. It was just for a few weeks. It was right before everything turned to shit." Sammy looked uncomfortable and was a little pale. He struggled in his seat to get up then he reached for Audrey. "Hey can you help me up? I gotta go to the john."

Audrey helped Sammy to his feet and steadied him on his walker. "You want me to come with you?"

"And wipe my ass? No thanks. I can do this. Just point me in the right direction."

He slowly made his way to the john as Audrey looked at him nervously wondering if she should go in there. The door shut behind him.

All this talk about family made Audrey sad. She thought about her family, or more like lack of family. She had been on her own most of her adult life. No kids, no parents, no real prospects. She opened up her purse to get a tissue, when her hand touched the burner phone that she had gotten Sammy.

She pulled it out and read the post-it note that Sammy had attached to the back: Barry (555) 727-9876.

She glanced once more at the door, then back at the phone.

Why not? she thought. She dialed the number and listened for the ring.

"Hello?" said Barry.

"Barry? Is this Barry?"

"Yeah. Who is this?"

"Okay. Listen. I don't have a lot of time but I just want to tell you that your dad is doing fine. I'm with him and we were just talking about you."

Barry interrupted. "My dad? Who the hell is this? Are you holding him somewhere that he can't leave?"

"What? No. He can leave. I mean I'm not holding him. He has a — well, a kinda bucket list of things he wants to do and that's all I can tell you. But I'm looking after him. I just wanted you to know."

"Why isn't he on the phone? Last time he called it was like he was reading a script. IS HE ALL RIGHT?"

"He is fine. He's in the bathroom. I know he will call you in the next day or so."

Barry thought about the caller and had a momentary feeling of relief. "Does he have everything he needs?"

"Yes. I think so. We just ate dinner and he, um, said the chicken sucked but other than being a pain in the ass he's got what he needs, I think."

Barry chuckled a little at the pain in the ass comment. "I'm glad he's okay. Thank you for calling. What's your name?"

"I'm Audrey. But please don't tell him we talked." She noticed Sammy heading back to the table. "Gotta go." She put the phone back in her purse.

Sammy slipped back into his seat as Audrey moved his walker.

"All okay?" She asked.

"Oh yeah. Just read that Bruce sucks dicks and Brandi is a whore."

"Well. You learn something new every day."

"I wrote down Brandi's phone number if you are interested."

"No thanks. I'm sure I work with her anyway."

"So," Sammy said, "where were we?"

"Oh. You were telling me about the girlfriend and things going to shit."

Sammy scratched his chin. "So the going to shit part was when the asshole I worked for stole money from the store and left me holding the bag. I went into bankruptcy and had to let the employees go."

"Oh no. ALL the employees?"

"All the employees. I had to let her go, too. Never saw her again. My brother Benny gave her a job at his pawn shop in Indiana. I was really young and really naive. And now I was broke, had to sell the house and had say goodbye forever to the woman I cared for so deeply. On top of that, Esther's mental health declined. "Sammy patted the urn. "We were never the same, were we, Miss Esther?" Sammy looked over at Audrey and smiled. "We can scratch off our third stop, Strippergirl."

"Ladies and Gentleman," the MC said into the microphone. "Welcome to the Corner Bar. We are going to kick things off with a classic guaranteed to bring back memories."

The solo banjo player strummed staccato chords and then sang the opening lyrics to, Do You Know What It Means To Miss New Orleans?

On the drive back, Sammy drifted off to sleep. Audrey glanced at him from time to time to make sure he was breathing. He didn't look well. He had a pasty color and hollow look in his face. She couldn't remember if he looked that way when she first met him.

It had only been less than a week but something kept gnawing at her about him. He was a crabby old guy, but there were the occasional times that he'd smile or say something funny and it would just warm her heart. She thought to herself, "I hope he doesn't die on my watch. What the hell would I do? I know nothing about him really. I don't even know his last name." The only saving grace was that she had connected with his son Barry, so now she had a name and number to call in an emergency.

Audrey pulled in to Rouses Market on Baronne. She loved that place and it was open until midnight. Lots of grab-and-go dinners just like eating at the big restaurants, except much cheaper. Sammy was not a big eater but she was and tonight she thought she'd splurge a little while he slept in the car.

"Hey, girlfriend. Where y'at?" A familiar voice spoke to her from behind a counter.

Audrey pointed at her in a high-sign gesture. "Hey, Paula baby. You workin' late, I see."

"Uh huh," Paula said, holding up her hands. "You see little piggies? Working them right down to the bone." They both shared a laugh. "What 'chu need, honey?"

Audrey pointed to the crawfish. "I'll do four pounds of the medium size." She looks at the shrimp, "And two pounds of those, please."

"You got it." Paula deftly scooped out the crawfish and wrapped them, writing the price on the paper and then did the same for the shrimp. She handed them over the counter to Audrey. "You take care of yourself."

"Thanks, Paula. See you soon." She then grabbed some bread, veggies, a few bottles of wine and hit the checkout line.

Outside, she put the bags in the trunk and then slipped in the front seat.

"Sammy?" Audrey dropped her keys when she looked at the passenger seat. Sam wasn't there. She looked in the back and it was empty as well. "Where the hell are you?"

She jumped out of the car, frantically looking up and down the street. There was nobody in sight for blocks. She ran to the corner, turned and ran another block looking in all directions and not seeing anyone. It was almost midnight. She went to the next block and did the same. "This is crazy," she thought. "I need to get in the car and drive around the neighborhood. That's what I'll do." She raced back to the car, jumped in and turned on the ignition.

"What did you get?" Sammy said from the passenger seat.

Startled, Audrey practically jumped out of her seat. She looked at Sammy in shock and relief. "Where the hell were you?"

"Bathroom." He said. "Got in just before they closed up."

"You scared the shit out of me. I didn't know where you went."

"Didn't know where you went either, when I woke up."

He said with his bottom lip extended. "But I figured it out."

Audrey frowned. "You sure go to the bathroom a lot."

"**D**o you know anyone named Audrey who works for you?" Barry asked Sidney Plotkin, the administrator at Star of David. Barry was sitting in front of Plotkin's desk.

"There are lots of Audreys here. I don't suppose she gave you a last name." Plotkin leaned in.

"No. Not even a hint. But she didn't sound too old. Maybe a nurse? A — volunteer?"

Plotkin picked up his phone and pushed a few buttons. "Sandy. Do me a favor, will you? Pull a list of everybody you can find who has the first name Audrey. Yes, that's right, Audrey. Oh, and volunteers as well. Right. Part-time, full-time … anytime. Former employees? Hold on." Plotkin looked at Barry, who nodded affirmatively. "Yes, former employees, too. Past five years."

"Thanks, Sid."

"Not a problem. We'll have it by tomorrow at the latest and then we'll give them all a call."

Barry sat back in his chair. "Good news is that this Audrey person cared enough to call and seems like she has his best interest at heart."

Plotkin walked over to the other side of the desk and placed his hand on Barry's shoulder.

"Barry, I can't tell you how sorry I am for everything that's happened. I accept full responsibility for this. You and I have known each other for so many years. I'm just sick about it."

"I know, Sid. You can sit down. I'm not going to sue you."

Plotkin stood straight. "In that case, let's go have lunch." He grabbed his wallet. "It's on me."

Barry stood as well. "Yes, it is."

SAMMY

DAY SIX

Paying Respects

As Sammy brushed his teeth, he noticed a calendar hanging next to the mirror. Audrey wrote little messages in the squares for each day: Hair — 3PM, Nails — 4:30, Rent due today. He looked at today's date and the note she had scribbled for today "pick up dry cleaning" was scratched out. Actually all the notes for the previous three days were scratched out as well. He wondered if that was because he was there and messed up her schedule completely. He smiled and looked ahead four days. His finger marked the date he had targeted for his last act, Sunday, August 4th. Esther would have been 80 on that date and he planned to grant her the one wish that escaped her when she was alive.

"Sammy. You almost done? My kidneys are bursting," Audrey screamed through the door.

He stepped out. "All yours — my dear."

"You're as bad as a woman."

"I have age that slows me down. Women have clutter."

Audrey closed the door on him.

S ammy dreaded the fourth stop on his list as he and Audrey drove down Canal Boulevard. We wouldn't stay long, he thought. But it was one he needed to do. As she pulled into Gates of Prayer Cemetery, Audrey felt a slight chill like she sometimes gets when she thinks about death and dying.

"I think it's the section to the right," Sammy said as he scanned the headstones, many of which were written in Hebrew. The graves were all underground and the headstones were plain and simple. They were very different from others in New Orleans. Jewish religious law required that members of the religion be buried below ground and headstones should reflect simple messages and not be too ornate, a trait that showed ostentatiousness and was frowned upon. "That's them, right under that tree."

Audrey pulled in to a space close by and helped Sammy out of the car. He gingerly walked the gravel path to the two gravesites and placed a stone on top of each headstone, a tradition that has its origins in the Bible. Many think it's a marker or tribute to show that there was a visitor. But there are deeper meanings, all somewhat different but all leading to the same conclusion. Stones are solid and remain with the departed and will never die (as flowers would). They also "keep the souls down" which would prevent the haunting of spirits after death.

The first held his father and his mother, Wolf and Fanny, placed side by side. There was no message, just an inscription of their names and dates of birth and death and a Star of David in the center. Their names were also written in Hebrew underneath.

Next to them was the gravesite of Michael Alan Levine. Inscribed below his name and birth/death were the words:

beloved son and beloved brother. Sammy whispered aloud, "Barry, I should have listened to you and put in the line 'and one helluva drummer.'"

He quietly recited the Mourner's Kaddish and stood in silence for a few minutes before he sat on the small bench located next to the path. Fanny lived for a long time, never really learned to speak English well and in her later years lived in a small room in sister Molly's house uptown. Wolf died young, early 40s and Sammy had very few real memories of him. He worked night and day repairing shoes just to make ends meet. Molly was buried close by in a double gravesite with her husband Morris. Benny, Sammy's older brother, is buried in Indianapolis with his wife Jeanette. He owned a little pawnshop and Sammy remembered him as the kindest, happiest man he ever met. Jeanette, on the other hand was the meanest.

He took out Esther's urn. "I know you don't want to be here. But I do. I just want you to know that I decided that I'm going to be buried right over there, between Michael and my mother. I know, I know, you hate to talk about burials. You didn't want to go underground and I kept my promise. I cremated you and that's that. No, I didn't argue with you I just wanted to make sure that's what you wanted to do. Jews don't get cremated. I know your parents did but your mother wasn't even Jewish. Let's not fight. I just thought you might want to visit Mikey one last time. It's hard on me, too."

From her sight line in the car, Audrey could only see Sammy's back and his gestures but she could tell he was yelling at Esther's urn.

When he finally stopped, his shoulders slumped and shook briefly as if he was quietly crying. He sat for another half hour until he lifted Esther into his back pack and shuffled back to the car.

There was no conversation on the ride back to Audrey's place. Sammy stared out the window, deep in thought.

A udrey wondered why the door was unlocked and the lights still on when stepped into her apartment. "It was probably Sally," she thought. "That girl is just unconscious about locking up and turning off the lights." Sammy was still making his way down the hall with his creaky old walker barely supporting him.

"Sally?" Audrey announced. "You here, girl? I see you left the door unlocked again."

From behind her, a hand closed around her mouth and pulled her head back to within an inch of a face that stunk of tobacco and alcohol. "Welcome home. Nice of Sally to leave a light on for me, huh?"

Audrey had a sick feeling in her stomach as she recognized the voice — and the smell. Zipline. The crazy bastard was in her apartment. She tried to scream at him but he just tightened his grip around her mouth. His other hand held a knife. It was the big carving knife that usually sat on the kitchen counter and it was right in front of her face so that she could plainly see it. "Things are a little different when somebody else has the knife. Huh, sugar?"

Audrey squirmed and grabbed his hand.

Zip forced his weight against her as he pushed her against the wall, knocking the air out of her lungs. He put the knife at her throat. "Cut that shit out. Relax or, I swear, I'll open up your neck right here and right now."

Sammy was in the doorway. "Hey! Leave her alone, you asshole."

Zip burst into laughter and turned Audrey around to face him, still covering her mouth. "No! Really? You still have your great grandfather with you? This is perfect." Zip moved Audrey closer to Sammy. "Diaper drawers. Sit over there in the Papa chair." He motioned to the overstuffed easy chair next to the couch. Sammy froze and just stood and stared at Zip. "You want I should cut your nursemaid here?" Sammy shook his head 'no.' "Then move it, Santa!"

Slowly, Sammy shuffled over to the chair, folded his walker and sat down.

Audrey's eyes were frantically scanning the apartment for something sharp or heavy or … "Take off your clothes and let's give Gramps a show you both will never forget." Zip pushed her against the closed door of the apartment. His hand was now on her throat and the other held the knife against her stomach. Audrey sneered at him. "Fuck you." She had her fists clenched, waiting for an opportunity to hit him in the throat, the balls or jab him in the eye.

"That's the general idea." Zip pushed gently on the knife and she felt the sharp blade against her stomach. Her fists relaxed for a second. "You don't remember how to take off your clothes? Let's see. Think back to … I don't know … EVERY NIGHT!" Zip was now right in her face hoarsely screaming the last words so that only those closest could hear. He pushed the knife further, which caused Audrey to whimper briefly.

She unbuttoned her blouse slowly. It was a very practiced move that she used on customers knowing it focused their attention on her boobs and caused momentary male paralysis of the brain. This time, it didn't work quite that way. Zip focused on her face. Pure hatred was in his eyes. It was the look of a cold-blooded killer sizing up his prey. She removed her blouse. Braless, her breasts were now in clear view.

"Everything. Keep going." Zip said in a steady voice.

Sammy sat helplessly looking at this horror show in front of him. He wondered how he could stop this. "You old fool," he thought to himself. He could try to grab the knife, maybe get killed in the process or just pushed aside.

Audrey was now down to her panties.

"Wait." Zip stopped her and said. "Take off my jeans."

She grabbed his belt buckle, still looking him in the eyes for any sign of brain freeze. Audrey unfastened his belt, opened his jeans buttons and slowly zipped down his fly. There it is, she thought. If she could reach inside and squeeze the shit out of his balls, maybe he would drop the knife.

"Hold it," Zip said. He grabbed her by the hair and bent her over the kitchen counter. "Pull down your panties."

She reached back and started to slide her panties down when Zip said, "What the hell?" He looked at the empty chair that held Sammy a couple of minutes ago. "Where is Grampa?" The toilet flushed and he switched his gaze to the bathroom door. Letting out a laugh, he focused once again on Audrey's body, bent over sensually. Her jaws tightened as she waited for the inevitable.

Zip felt a tap on his shoulder. "What the fuck, old man?" he said, still looking at Destiny's ass, "Do you need me to wipe you now?" As he spoke, he turned to look at Sammy, but instead stared right into a thick spray of bleach that Sammy pointed right at his eyes. Zip screamed in pain and covered his eyes.

He swatted Sammy, who fell against the oven, throwing back the bottle of bleach but maintained his balance, miraculously.

At the same time, Audrey reached for a fork from the sink, turned and stabbed him in the hand holding the knife. He screamed again and dropped the knife at her feet. She picked it up and went for his throat.

Sammy held her arm back. "Don't do it."

Audrey instinctively pulled away from Sammy and was inches away from slashing Zip's throat. He was temporarily blinded and swatting at the air around him. She stopped and looked at the pathetic animal in front of her. She kicked him in the crotch and as he lay there clutching his balls, she kicked him in the face.

"Much better choice," Sammy said. Zip writhed and moaned on the ground as Audrey picked up Sammy's walker and helped him to right himself. He was leaning against the oven and was covered with baking powder that had exploded when he knocked it over. It was all over his glasses and his windbreaker. She laughed slightly as she brushed him off. "You are my hero, Mr. Finkelstein."

Zip's eyes cleared slightly and seeing that Audrey was out of range, he scampered on all fours to the door and pushed it open, running down the hall to safety.

"Chickenshit," Audrey said as Sammy smiled.

"Well, that was an unexpected adventure. Maybe I'll list that as number five."

"Maybe we just call it a night." Audrey helped Sammy into bed and made a mental note to call one of her friends at NOPD in the morning.

SAMMY

DAY SEVEN

Strip Bowling

"**D**id you sleep okay?" Audrey asked Sammy as she bit into a puffy beignet, creating a small cloud of powdered sugar around her mouth. They sat together at Café Du Monde in the middle of a crowd of sweaty tourists squeezed into tiny seats on the patio. The tourists waited patiently in line for an empty table. Not the natives. They slip in and sit when someone leaves even if the table is dirty.

"No. I really don't sleep anymore." Sammy said as he motioned to one of the Asian waiters in an old white paper waiter cap and little black bowtie.

"Seemed like you were dead to the world last night when I heard you snoring."

"That's just a power nap." Sammy said.

The Asian waiter scurried over to the table. "Sir?"

"This coffee is not hot." Sammy pointed to his cup. "I want it really hot. Understand? And black, not with milk, okay? "

"Yes, understand. Sorry." He grabbed the cup and disappeared.

Sammy shook his head and leaned in to talk to Esther's urn, which sat prominently in the center of the table.

"Nothing's changed here. They still bring the coffee lukewarm. I gotta tell them every time."

Audrey talked to Esther too. "No café au lait for Sammy boy. Huh?"

"I don't drink milk in my coffee. That screws it up." Sammy grumbled. "Esther liked café au lait. Can't taste the chicory though."

Audrey patted him on the shoulder. "This is either a favorite place that you love to hate or not on your bucket list."

"This one's for Esther. She loved this place. Well, actually she loved Morning Call. You were probably too young to remember that place. It was a block or two that way." Sammy pointed past the market. "They moved the whole damned place to Metairie. In a strip center. Hah! Insides still look the same. Outside looks like a Kmart or something."

"I know where it is. Big mirrors right?"

"Yep. That's it."

Audrey looked at her phone. "Sally texted me."

"Oh she did, huh?" Sammy answered. "Did she apologize for leaving the door unlocked?"

Audrey put the phone back in her bag. "She did."

"None of my business, but I think you should be careful who has access to your apartment keys."

"You're right. It isn't any of your business."

He held up his hands. "So, how did that crazy bastard know where you lived."

Audrey silently drank her coffee.

Sammy continued. "No. You didn't. You brought him there before?"

Audrey looked away.

"Audrey. You slept with that asshole?"

She looked at him. "No. I didn't sleep with him." She took another sip. "Sally did. Last year."

"Sally did. I see."

Audrey glared at him. "Okay. She has really shitty taste in men and piss poor judgment."

"You think?" Sammy said.

The waiter brought a fresh cup of coffee that literally was smoking. Sammy sipped it as the waiter waited. Sammy nodded and shooed him away. The waiter did a slight bow and left. "Still not hot enough," Sammy told Sally.

Audrey's phone played a few chords of Katy Perry's I Kissed A Girl. She answered. "Hello. Yes. Oh, hello, Detective Kirby." Sammy tried to hear, too. "Everybody just calls him Zipline. He's a real piece of work. Well ... like I told the officer this morning, he was in the apartment when we got there. He attacked me and my friend sprayed his eyes with bleach and I stabbed him with a fork." Sammy laughed. "My friend's name?" Sammy waved his hands and mouthed the word "no." "Finkelstein. Ira Finkelstein. He's an old man I been taking care of for a few days." She looked at him. "No, he wasn't hurt. Me either." She took a napkin and took out a pen and wrote down a number. "I will. Thanks." Audrey put the napkin in her bag and closed it up. She sighed and looked at Sammy.

"You okay?" he asked.

She nodded her head. "Been through worse."

Sammy looked to his right as the street tap dancers were showing their stuff to the tourists. Young boys in wifebeater tee shirts, oversized jeans and big sneakers with huge metal taps screwed into the soles were dancing out rhythms that were truly impressive. The noise of their taps was so loud that you could barely hear yourself talk.

Sammy let out a laugh.

"What's so funny, Sammy Boy?"

"Just thinking about my boys when they were little and used to come here with me on Saturday mornings."

"Thought Esther didn't like this place."

"She didn't. But Barry and Mikey and I would come here for breakfast before the store opened on days that I brought them in with me." Sammy said. "Mikey used to stare at the street performers the whole time. Just fascinated. I would tell him to finish his milk and pay less attention to the kids on the street. One day, he asked me, 'Daddy, do those kids live there?' I told him that they had homes like we do and they came out every day to do what they do just like we go to work. Barry asked if I would give him a dollar so he could put it in their bucket. I told him no. It was all a scam. Look how stupid the tourists are giving these kids money for that foolish business. 'But it's their job, isn't it?' Barry asked me 'That's what you said.'"

"What did you tell Barry?"

"I don't remember. Or maybe I chose to forget. Barry was always the arguer. Not satisfied with the simple answer. He was the more complicated of the two boys. He was more like Esther. He was very smart and talented."

"Did you ever tell him that?"

"That he was smart and talented? Oh sure. I guess I did."

"Mikey was your favorite, right?"

"Why? Because he didn't argue as much?"

"Because he was more like you."

Sammy gave Audrey a big squeeze. "You are pretty smart yourself for a stripper."

"Barry's worried about you."

"I know. I know."

"Why didn't you tell him where you were?"

"I actually did tell him, in a way."

"But I thought you told him ..."

He interrupted. "I told him I didn't want him to take me back and mess up my plans."

"I'm confused." Audrey sipped her coffee.

"Before I left, I gave Barry an envelope. I told him in the envelope was a note that was very important to me and I wanted him to open it when he was alone. In the note, I told him my plans for the last day here."

"What did he say?"

"About the note? Nothing. He didn't read it. He probably thought it was like my other notes to him where I put down shopping lists and stuff."

"So why don't you just TELL HIM instead of playing this stupid game."

Sammy was quiet for a while and just said, "It's complicated."

Finally, Audrey put down her coffee and held out her hand to Sammy. "Hey. Let me see your bucket list."

Sammy carefully removed his bucket list piece of paper from his shirt pocket and handed it to Audrey. She looked at the remaining items that weren't scratched out, pointed to her favorite and said, "Let's do this one."

"You ready for another one?" Jenny smiled seductively, as she wiped down the bar in front of Barry's beer bottle. BJ's was quiet. There were only about six other customers scattered around. Two old beach guys played darts, a couple in the corner were cemented together in the booth, old Frankie was asleep at the end of the bar and Flip was taking a leak in the men's room.

"Sure, why not?" He pushed his empty bud bottle toward Jenny's outstretched hand. She stuck a finger through the hole and flipped it in the trash can. She reached down in the bin below the bar and offered Barry a spectacular view of her healthy cleavage.

"The twins look lovely tonight, Jen." Barry said as he took a sip of the fresh Bud that Jenny handed him.

"They miss you, baby." Jenny gave him a selfie pout as she seductively moved to the other end of the bar to serve one of the dart players. Barry watched her move. Why hadn't he called her in a while? He had such a good time with her and it certainly wasn't because the sex wasn't great. The mirror behind the bar depressed him. Who was that old guy looking at him? He looked tired, bored and had no interest in life.

"Are we looking at how sexy we are?" Flip put his face right next to Barry's and gave a wide grin in the mirror.

Barry pushed his head away. "Sexy, huh? I was just thinking how much I'm starting to look like my old man."

"Sammy? The women LOVE Sammy."

"Oh yeah ... just about as much as getting their legs waxed."

As if on cue, Barry's phone sang out I Just Called To Say I Love You. He looked down and UNKNOWN appeared on the screen. He stared at it.

"Answer it, man!"

Barry grabbed it up quickly and ran outside. Taking a chance he said, "Dad? Dad?"

Sammy's gravelly voice answered. "Hello. Barry?"

"Dad. Are you alright?"

"You ask me that a lot, you know?"

"You could be dead."

"Would be hard to have a two-way conversation if I was." There was a moment of silence where both of them were searching for words. Sammy continued. "Barry. Do you remember when I used to take you bowling?"

Barry's brow wrinkled. "Yeah, I remember."

"You used to always want to use my ball."

"I loved that ball," Barry remembered. "It had gold flecks and swirls and it was emerald green with a big gold SAMMY on it." He laughed at the thought.

"You would drag that ball with both hands right up to the line and push it as hard as you could down the lane. You didn't care how heavy it was or how much harder it would be to hit the pins. You just wanted to throw that ball. I used to say, 'Barry use a lighter one,' but you said you just wanted to use that one. Remember?"

"Yes. I remember." Barry finished his thought surprising himself with his honesty. "I wanted to be just like you."

Sammy stopped for a moment to wipe his eyes. "You never gave up. And there was Mikey, clapping for you so loud when the ball finally hit the pins."

"One pin, if I got lucky and it didn't go in the gutter." Barry said.

Sammy continued, "I bought you a ball with your name on it when you were older but I don't think you ever used it. Didn't you like it?"

"When I was in high school, having a bowling ball with your name on it was pretty dorky." Barry said. "Actually, going bowling was kinda dorky."

"Do you ever go bowling now?"

Barry thought about it. "Haven't really bowled in years."

"Did you ever take Wendy?"

"Wendy didn't really like bowling. She was into soccer and then boys and then shopping and then more boys."

They both laughed.

"Take her bowling sometime, Barry."

Barry smiled. "How about I take you and Wendy bowling one night."

"I'd like that, son."

"Let's do it ... tomorrow!"

"Soon. I still have stuff to do." Sammy remembered something. "Hey, remember my lucky hat?"

"The goofy one that you caught at one of the parades that said, 'Throw me something Mister?'"

"Yeah. That one. Your mom hated it. She tried to throw it out so many times."

"Too bad you stopped her."

"You know where that hat is?"

Barry thought about it. "There's a big box of your shit in the storage shed. It might be there. Your bowling ball might be too."

"Can you check for me?"

"I will." Barry took out a cigarette and lit it. "Dad, is that Audrey girl still taking care of you? Are you coming back soon?"

"Yes and yes."

"Will you just tell me where you are?"

Sammy looked out the window at the streets of the French Quarter. "I wanted to tell you and even started to tell you a couple of weeks ago. But I didn't want you to talk me out of it or make me stay."

"But ..."

"Bye, son. I'll be finished in just a couple of days." He looked down. "You should really try these burner phones sometime."

Sammy was gone.

Barry still held the phone to his ear.

"Love you too, Sammy."

Sammy knocked on Audrey's bedroom door. "Hey. Are you ready? According to my watch, I'm gonna be dead before you get your teeth brushed. So shake it Strippergirl."

Audrey swung the door open with a flourish. "TA DA!"

Sammy looked at her pink shirt. It had "Strippergirl" screened in rainbow colors across her breasts. "You like?" she asked.

"Cute," Sammy said dryly.

"Well, check this out." She turned and held out her arms. On the back were the words "Sammy's Ballers" screaming out in bright green, framed by two enormous cartoon bowling balls . "What do you think about that?"

He laughed loudly. "Well I'll be a dirty old bastard. Very clever." He scratched his chin. "But grammatically incorrect. There is only one baller."

"Nope. We got lots of them." Audrey stepped aside and three more girls stepped out into the living room. Each had bright pink shirts with their names across the front: Mustang Sally, The Schwartze and Mercedes. They, of course, had the same team name as Audrey, Sammy's Ballers. "We all decided to join you on your next bucket list adventure — if that's okay with you, of course."

"Sounds like a plan. I'm honored to have you all on my team."

Sally handed Sammy a package. "Yo, big daddy. You can't really be our fearless leader without this."

He smiled. "It ain't my birthday, Sally." He snapped off the pink bow and ripped into the paper. When he lifted the lid he reached in and pulled out a pink shirt — this one had buttons and looked more like a traditional bowling shirt. On the front pocket, it was inscribed "Captain" and the back had "Sam I Am" written over the two bowling balls.

The girls all applauded as he put his new shirt on and took a bow. "Thank you, girls. This must have cost you a fortune."

"Would have if we used our own money, Mr. Finkelstein." she winked. "and wait. There's more." Audrey reached down and took out a big giftwrapped box and Mercedes grabbed a long, skinny one. They both handed them to Sammy.

"Mine first," said Mercedes.

Sammy ripped away the skinny wrapping and unveiled a brand new metal cane with a base. "It's called a quad cane. We got it at CVS. What do you think?"

Sammy carefully got to his feet and balanced himself with the cane. The four "feet" of the base held steady. "Not bad. I like it."

"Okay, next one." Audrey said.

The girls could hardly contain themselves as they hurried him and even helped rip open the paper on the big box, finally revealing a pink bowling ball bag with rainbow letters spelling out "Esther's Got a Brand New Bag." He smiled and reached down to pick up Esther's urn from the living room table and gently placed it into the bowling bag.

"Perfect!" He said as he opened the door. "Ladies, let's roll!"

Mid-City Lanes is located in the center of New Orleans on Carrolton Avenue and has been there since 1941. Sammy bowled there regularly with his buddies from team B'nai Brith. Wednesday night was league night at Mid-City and the serious bowlers were always there. Those were the days when scoring was done by hand and lists of the top teams and high scorers were taped and tacked to the walls.

Trophies of all sizes and shapes were in display racks and almost every

Bowler carried his own bowling ball bag. It was as if Tony Soprano, Paulie, Silvio and the gang were cloned and clothed in different color bowling shirts and played on every team.

Sammy hung with Izzy, Smitty, Seymore and Bert but they looked like the Sopranos, too. Team names went from the standard King Pins or Lucky Strike to more creative Split Happens or Here 4 the Beer. The women also had teams. They had names like Dangerous Dames or Gutter Girls or my favorite, Dolls With Balls. They kinda looked like Tony Soprano, too ... just with bigger hair.

Mid-City was sold in the late 80's and soon afterward changed the name to Rock'n' Bowl. Over the years, it became more of a live music and bar venue with a huge dance floor on one side and the lanes on the other. The leagues still played but were smaller and played less often. Sammy's team slowly faded away with bowlers dying off and venues taken over by a different audience.

Today was Sammy's first day back to Mid-City in more than 20 years.

When Sammy's Ballers hit the front door of Rock'n Bowl, all eyes were on the pink shirted bowlers (and the short skirts, knee highs, garter stockings and heels).

Layla (aka "The Schvartze") ran over to Lane 6, clomping up to the ball holder with her platform heels. "Let's play here! Girl! Look at these big old purple balls." She cradled one and stepped right up to the line.

"Wait, Layla!" Audrey screamed. Too late, as Layla threw the ball forward, making it bounce down the lane and causing her to fall backward on her butt. Audrey and the team raced over to her and picked her up from the floor. "What the hell are you thinking? You gotta sign in and get some bowling shoes and then we get a lane ..."

Layla looked to her right at the group of senior citizens gathered around her, gawking. "Those nasty shoes?" She pointed at their feet. "No, uh-uh, I ain't putting my feet in those things. I'm wearing my own, baby."

Mercedes chimed in. "I told you when we got to Audrey's, didn't I? I said no drama. No drama tonight. We gonna work as a team."

"Shut up Mercedes before I knock you upside your fluffy ass head."

Sally added, "I gotta agree with Layla. Those shoes are an easy 10 on the ugly scale."

"We are in a bowling alley." Audrey said. "It's not like we're going to a damn party."

The girls were now circling each other trying to hold back Layla and keep Mercedes under control too. Just then, Sammy scooted up to the group balancing five pairs of bowling shoes in his right arm. "Are we having fun yet?" They all turned to look at Sammy and the crowd that gathered behind him.

Layla walked up to a balding man who was about 5-foot-2 and held a bowling ball to his chin. "What'chu looking at?"

"This is our lane," he said meekly.

"Well excuse me!" She huffed past him and grabbed a pair of shoes.

Mid-City Rock'n Bowl came alive with lights and music as soon as the Ballers checked in at lane ten. The girls were giddy now as they picked out their brightly colored balls, finally settled on which bowling shoes they wanted to wear and picked their positions to bowl.

"Sammy, you want to go first?" Sally asked.

"Ladies first. I'll watch and help any one that needs it." Truth was, Sammy was feeling a little stiff and had that shooting pain in his shoulder. Better to just sit and wait, he thought.

"I'll go." Audrey spoke up and balanced the ball as she stood at the line.

"Hey Strippergirl," Sammy yelled. "Stand about three feet back and walk up to the line when you are rolling the ball like this." He demonstrated with an imaginary ball shuffling three steps while swinging his right arm.

"Do I have to shuffle like an old man when I do it?"

Sammy flipped her a bird and sat down.

"Okay here goes." Audrey said as she took three steps and rolled the ball. A turtle could have caught up with it as it gradually plopped into the gutter.

"That's okay, honey," Layla said. "You looked pretty doin' it."

Sammy laughed. He stood up and balanced on his cane. "I'm gonna check out the men's room." Then he headed to the front desk. A tall pimple-faced adolescent wiped down the counter as Sammy stepped up. "Say, son, does a Walter Smith work here?"

"Yes sir. He's probably in the equipment room polishing bowling balls right about now."

"Where's that?"

"Um, third door on your right. Not marked but you'll see it."

Sammy walked past the dividing line between the lanes and the big dance floor where a zydeco band played Cajun music to the crowd of "coon ass" rednecks (as they were lovingly called by their peers). He pushed open the door to the equipment room and there was Walter Smith, his former young employee at Holtzman's whom he mentored and took care of when he was just a teenager. Walter still had his tiny moustache and "cookie duster," as Walter called it, below his lower lip. But the facial hair was grayer now and a stark contrast to his dark skin, drawn and wrinkled with the passage of time. He was wearing a one-piece blue uniform with the Rock'n Bowl logo on the back.

"Walter?" Sammy asked. "That you?"

Walter paused and peered over his glasses at Sammy. He put down his polishing cloth and stepped closer. "Mr. Sam?"

Sammy nodded yes.

"Well as I live and breathe. I ain't seen you in what — 30 years or so?"

"That's probably right." Sammy said. "I hoped you were still here. You're on my bucket list."

Walter gave Sammy a big hug, careful not to squeeze too hard. "I am honored, Mr. Sam. Yeah, I have been here for about 40 years I guess on and off." Walter smiled. "How's Miss Esther?"

Sammy held up the bowling ball bag he was carrying and showed Walter the urn. "Unfortunately, she passed a few years back."

"I'm so sorry," Walter said.

"We all are here for such a short time." He looked at the urn. "I know she would be so happy to see you, Walter."

Walter moved some papers off a folding chair. "Sit, sit. Lemme look at you, Mr. Sam." He studied him. "Looking good!"

"Liar! I look like shit." Sammy smirked. "You too."

Walter laughed. "Well you haven't changed, that's for sure."

"Was thinking about you this morning coming down here. I remembered when I found you crouched in the corner of my store, hiding from the NOPD, with a bunch of candy bars and cigarettes in your pockets."

"I think about that time in my life a lot." He sat across from Sammy. "You saved my life, you know? Giving me a job, buying me clothes and stuff when I needed them."

"And calling your mother to give your ass a whupping for stealing shit."

Walter put his head back and laughed loudly. "That too."

Sammy looked around the room. "I also remember when you said you were ready to be on your own and started working here. It was when I lost the business." Sammy looked down at the floor. "I let so many people down."

"Stop it." Walter said. "You never let nobody down. Actually, working here, having to rely on myself ... changed my life."

Sammy put his hand on Walter's shoulder. "You have a family now?"

"Sure do. Beautiful wife, two boys who live right here in New Orleans and have families of their own. I'm a blessed man."

Just then, the pimpled-faced boy popped in and handed Walter a piece of paper. "The guys from AMF just got here."

"Thanks, Reggie."

Sammy stood. "Hey, is Willy still around?"

"No. Willy sold the place in the '80s."

"Who bought it?"

"Me." Walter said.

Sammy stopped. "No way." He continued. "Wait a minute. What the hell are you doing polishing balls? Don't you have people to do that?"

"I like polishing balls." Walter leaned closer. "I polish them at my other five bowling alleys, too."

Walter put his arm around Sammy. "What do you think of your schvartze ganif now?"

Sammy laughed. "Think? I think I might be able to bowl for free today."

By the time that Sammy returned to lane 10, his team had just about taken over the entire bowling alley. Bowlers from different teams were lining up to give them lessons, share beers and watch them dance to the zydeco music. The other women bowlers however were not so happy with their neighbors. Standing firmly with hands on hips, one of the women bowlers scrutinized Mustang Sally as she watched her husband carefully show her how to hold her ball. "Let her hold yours first, Tony. It's so much smaller and easier to manipulate!" Mrs. Tony remarked.

"Sammy!" Audrey called to Sammy as he came up to the lane. "Where have you been? We have been waiting for you. Did we ruin your bucket list?"

"No. No. In fact this may have been the best one ever." He reached over and grabbed one of the bowling balls that seemed like the right fit and weight. His shoulder still hurt but was no longer causing intense discomfort. "Let's see if I still have it."

Audrey got everyone's attention — "Girls! Our fearless leader is here to show us how it's done."

Almost in unison the girls started to chant, "Sammy! Sammy!"

Sammy stood on his favorite arrow on the floor corresponding to the number 6 pin on the right. He cradled the ball in the crook of his right arm as he stabilized himself on his cane. He took a deep breath. He started his familiar walk but stopped after two steps. "Different with a cane." He laughed. He backed up and started again, this time making it to the line and lowering the ball. But the ball slipped out of his fingers and dribbled over to the lane next to him. The bowler to his right stopped and grabbed the wandering ball for Sammy.

"Here you go, oldtimer. Maybe a lighter ball will help." The bowler commented.

Sammy fumed at the remark. So did his teammates. He managed a "No, thank you. This ball seems fine." With that, Sammy took his stance, the girls resumed their chant, "Sammy! Sammy!" and he shuffled down to the line. This time Sammy felt a little of the old familiar arm action that had once made him one of the best in town. He snapped the wrist slightly at the end of his throw, putting English on the approach. It travelled slowly, not like the old days when he could zip it down the lane. But it had enough speed to make the curve. It landed right in the pocket between the No.#1 and the No.#3 pins and they all fell with a flourish.

The bowler to his right stopped to watch and politely applauded as the crowd went wild, screaming his name and flipping off the other bowler who so rudely put him down. Sammy smiled and accepted lots of high fives. While all this was going on, Walter came up to Lane 10 holding a large trophy in his hand. "Mr. Sam! I was just coming up to show you what I found and caught your stellar strike!"

Sammy looked down at it and noticed it was an old one that was inscribed: "First Place B'nai Brith Bombers. High Series Score: Sammy Levine, 879."

"Is that you?" Mercedes asked.

"That's me. On a lucky day." Sammy felt pressure in his chest. His breathing was more shallow.

"Know what?" Walter said to the girls. "I think I'll put this out again. Right over there in the trophy case by the front door. How about that Mr. Sam?"

Sammy's knees buckled as he collapsed on the floor.

It had to be 90 degrees, Barry thought as he lumbered down the beach on Pass-a-Grille. He was right. It was actually 92 and the usual breeze that came off the water was hot and steamy, not cool and relaxing.

He passed a virtual menagerie of beach people of every shape, size, color and species. There was the white, translucent couple from Toronto with their babies playing in the sand (sporting those inflatable arm life preservers). Their skin would be bright red by the end of the afternoon. Did they not read the book about skin cancer, ever? Two women under a massive tent weighed in at an easy 300 pounds apiece. They wore bathing suits with plunging necklines and frilly skirts. A cooler the size of Texas sat between them, certainly filled with 30 pounds of ribs and beer. An older, leather-skinned man with a large-brimmed hat passed by Barry. On closer look, he wasn't much older than Barry. But the sun has a way of keeping score. A gaggle of teens threw frisbees and footballs in the sand. The girls were all legs and the guys were all testosterone.

Barry's knees were aching and his head was splitting but he continued on. Running was not really his forte, but he decided he needed a stress reliever to balance out the prior week. Sammy going missing in action was bad enough; but the bills that were mounting up at the office were making him rethink his entire music career. The studio jobs were getting tougher to find. When he left the ad agency, Barry thought he could find a ton of work now that the technology made it simple to cut tracks and email them to fellow musicians to mix. But the recording industry was going through massive changes. Musicians were back on the road performing to make money. Songs were the byproduct instead of the end product and times were tough.

So, bad knees and all, Barry ran his stress out on the beach. Better than the casino, he thought. Not a healthy habit, Karen used to tell him before she finally got fed up and left him. He spent hours at the tables and on the machines pouring money he didn't have into that giant funnel. He gave the gambler's pledge every time he went. "I promise not to go any more." He had also started smoking again. It was just another great habit that he had kicked 20 years ago and now seemed like the intelligent thing to do.

His divorce and Mikey's death happened at about the same time. Wendy was his saving grace. Being a good dad motivated him to not go over the dark side. But he did a good job of skirting the edges.

This week was tough.

His phone rang. It was Dave Goldman.

"Hey, shithead. What are you doing?" Dave asked as Barry stopped to talk to him.

"Discovering new ways to reduce stress."

"Oh. You getting stoned?"

"No, dumbass. I'm running on the beach."

"Really?" Dave asked. "That works?"

"I'll tell you as soon as I get rid of this guy on the phone that creates stress."

"Well, my friend." Dave said. "Just so happens that old DG is your answer to reducing stress the old fashioned way, by making some money this weekend."

Barry sat down and stared at the water. "Really?"

"Really. I got a gig in New Orleans and need a keyboard player this weekend. I know it's short notice but I thought I'd ask my CHOSEN buddy."

"This weekend? As in which day?"

"Saturday night. It's a place in the Quarter ... a buddy is getting married and it's his wedding party."

"Can I tell you tomorrow? I gotta move some stuff around."

"Like doing your wash and grocery shopping? I need you, man."

Barry smiled. "I was supposed to do something with Wendy. It's her birthday." Barry said. "I'll talk to her."

"Okay, let me know."

Bright lights came into focus as Sammy squinted. "Am I dead?"

"Not yet." He recognized Audrey's voice. "But I'll be happy to give it a shot."

Sammy turned to see Audrey standing over him with her fist clenched. He was lying on a cot in the warehouse of the bowling alley. Walter smiled at his feet.

"Why didn't you tell anyone you were having chest pains?"

"How did you know I was?"

"Because you grabbed your heart and screamed when you passed out." Audrey turned to the wall. "Look, Sammy. I offered to help you with this whole bucket list thing because I thought, I don't know, that it was sweet and you are like a crusty old asshole without friends who needed my help."

"That's reassuring," Sammy said.

"But I'm not gonna be responsible for you dying on me. I don't need that shit."

"Who said you have to be responsible for that?"

Audrey got in his face. "I did! You have to tell me when it's too much. SHIT! I should have never helped you get out of the hospital. I am taking you back. This is too much."

"No. Just three more days. I promise. That's all I need."

Walter chimed in. "She's right, Mr. Sam. You have heart problems, I heard the doctor told you, right? He wanted you to stay at the hospital."

Sammy sat up. "I'm fine. I just got a little winded from bowling that's all." He grabbed Audrey's hand. "Please, Audrey, just let me stay the rest of the week and I'll be out of your hair forever. If I feel the least bit sick or in pain I'll go back to the hospital. I promise."

"Okay. But don't die on me! Or I'll kill you."

Sammy laid his head back on the Mustang's passenger seat headrest and thought about his plan for the next few days. He needed more time but he couldn't afford to wait. Sunday was Esther's birthday and he had to be finished by then. He had been planning this for such a long time.

Each stop was important and only he and Esther knew why.

The first stop was the Sazerac. Sure, he couldn't get a room at the Roosevelt but he had the drink at the bar and slipped a memento into his pocket when Caesar wasn't looking. It was a bar menu, bound in leather but certainly not going to be missed by anyone important.

Next was Silk Stockings, the strip club. There were two reasons for that stop. His first visit to a real strip club — and Audrey. In due time, he would reveal to Audrey why she was so important to him but in the meantime, he had slipped a pack of matches and a garter belt from the dressing room into his knapsack.

Then came the fishing trip and his old friend Dickie Broussard. Dickie fell right into his trap almost too easily. What could he take to remember that afternoon? Well, after he made the phone call to the Feds, he slipped back to the desk. Dickie must have gone to take a piss and left his pinky ring (with a sapphire in the middle). That also wound up in the knapsack. Dickie certainly wouldn't need it where he was going.

The Jazz Club followed. Actually, it was the site of his old furniture store that he was after. He confessed of his transgressions there to Esther. He told Audrey he needed to visit the john but he really slipped outside to remove one of the old tiles from the side of the building, which came off easily. It was brittle and cracked.

The Gravesite visit the next day was even more emotional. He relived the conversations with Esther about burial vs. cremation and he confronted his depressed feelings about Mikey.

He took three stones from the ground, one from each site: His mother, father, and son Michael.

Mid-City Lanes was still fresh on his mind. What a treat seeing Walter Smith. He was and still is the best human being he ever met, Sammy thought. He would give you the shirt off his back. He did, in fact. Well, actually Sammy lifted it from one of the shelves of his storeroom. It had Walter's name embroidered right on the pocket.

"What are you smiling about?" Audrey asked.

"Just reliving our adventures, Strippergirl."

"Doesn't take much to make you happy, Sammy." Audrey lit a cigarette and blew smoke out the window. "So where are we going tomorrow?"

"Not we. Me. I've got to do this one alone."

"Woah there, big fella. How you gonna get there?"

"I'll take one of those Y-ubers"

"UBERS?"

"Yeah that's what I meant."

"Sorry. Not gonna happen. What if you drop dead and nobody is around?"

"The UBER guy would be."

Audrey punched him playfully in the arm. "I'll drive you and wait for you in the car."

"But, you don't even know where I'm going. What if it's someplace that you can't go to like it's off limits to women."

"Is this place off limits to women?"

"No."

"Then I'm driving."

Wendy checked her phone for the third time in the last fifteen minutes.

"Why does he always keep me waiting?" she thought as she took another sip of her Chardonnay. Italia Mia was packed tonight. She felt super guilty about sitting in the booth for four, feeling like all eyes were on her and she should just stand up and say, "No I'm not selfishly keeping this booth for myself. My dad is coming soon, I hope."

Every now and then, Pina would come by and say, "Would you like more wine, Miss Wendy?" He should call. He should just give me that. Wendy fiddled again with her phone, this time texting him "Where R U?"

A hand reached over and patted her shoulder. "Hey your papa ... he at the casino you think?"

Wendy laughed and looked at Tony and said, "You would know before I know."

"No way. I haven't been in, I dunno, two months." Wendy looked at Carla, Tony's wife, behind the counter. She shook her head "no" and raised her palms in the air.

"Not what Carla says, Tony."

"Ahhh, she don't know. That place take all my money." Tony picked up her glass. "You want more wine?"

"Sure."

Wendy and Barry frequented Italia Mia at least twice a month. It's their "date night" on Thursdays and they rarely miss one. Well, Barry is rarely on time, but he tries to never miss it completely. It was his favorite night out.

Pina filled Wendy's glass.

"There he is." Tony bellowed from the kitchen. Barry waved to him as he wound his way through the maze of tables to find Wendy, now glaring at him over her glasses.

"I know, sweetheart. I'm so sorry. Last-minute charts and I lost track of time. Do you forgive me?" He kissed her sweetly on the top of her head.

"No." She took a big gulp of wine. "At least Tony and Pina have been keeping me company. And keeping me loopy too." She lifted up the wine glass. "This is number three I think or maybe four."

"Whoa. Slow down, little girl. You're gonna need lots of coffee."

Pina came over. "Hi Mr. Barry. You want-a some wine before dinner?"

"Sure Pina. The Cab, please."

"Ok. And you want-a the usual for your meals tonight?"

Barry looked over at Wendy who smiled and nodded.

Pina said, "Okay then. I'll bring-a you some bread to start."

"Thanks, Pina." Barry quickly checked his phone for any messages and spread his napkin on his lap.

"Any more from Grampy, dad?" Wendy asked.

"I got the strangest call from him last night."

"He called you? What did he say?"

"It was all about bowling."

"Bowling?"

"Yeah. Bowling. He wanted to know if I remembered the times we bowled together." Barry smiled.

"Did you go bowling a lot with Grampy?"

"Actually, I did when I was younger. He would take me to a place called Mid-City with his buddies and we would bowl for hours. I was thinking about him today. You know, bowling was one of the things that we shared … maybe the only thing we shared together. Grampy and I didn't really do much together. I have to admit, I loved our bowling nights. He reminded me of how I used to love to use his big green bowling ball with the gold specks. The thing was huge and heavy and I struggled just to get it balanced in my hands. But I only wanted to use that ball. On those nights, I wanted to be just like him. Other nights, not so much."

"We should go bowling some night."

He gave out a little laugh. "That's what he said. But you hate bowling."

"I used to hate the IDEA of bowling. Now I think it's pretty cool." Wendy took a sip. "And, maybe you should have a date night with Grampy like we do."

"He's not a fun date like you are."

"Oh sure. That's why you keep me waiting for hours."

"Hours?"

"Seems like." Wendy grinned.

Pina brought over some bread and oil. She refilled the wine. "Food will be out soon."

"He called me too." Wendy said out of the blue.

"What? Grampy called you?" Barry leaned in.

"Yes. He called me last night."

"From his burner phone, he told me." They both laughed.

"What did he say?"

"He missed me and I'm his favorite," Wendy made a little halo with her fingers and put them over her head. "The usual."

"Brat. So you think he sounded okay?"

"Actually, I think he sounded really tired. But I think he's really happy, you know?"

"Yes, I know. I think so too, honey. Wherever he is, he is doing exactly what he wants to do and that makes me feel okay."

Wendy patted Barry on the hand.

Pina returned with two plates of chicken cacciatore and ziti. As it was served, Barry commented to Pina: "Tell Tony that this looks so spectacular I know he didn't cook it."

"He no make-a the food ever. He only make-a the trouble!" They all share a laugh and looked over at Tony who shrugged his shoulders.

"So, tell me about you. How's the new job?" Barry asked.

"Great. I like my boss. I like what I'm doing and I have no complaints."

"Working on any interesting projects?"

"Um, not yet but getting there. I am helping on a campaign to clean up the shorelines. I went to a meeting with my boss to talk to the group of guys who are working to fund it. They live on St. Pete Beach. Funny name ... SOBs. Stands for Sons of the Beaches. They meet at a little motel and are part of the Rotary Club. There's some senator involved. Anyway, I'm starting to write the copy."

"Sounds great."

They took a few bites of cacciatori and enjoy dinner together. Barry looked at Wendy with pride. He was so happy that he could finally hear the words "I like what I'm doing."

"So, how's the music biz daddio?"

"Hummin' along."

"What have you written lately?"

Barry swallowed hard. "Just a few commercial tags and some interstitials. Been working on a few tunes that I'll play for you sometime. Just for myself, you know? And there's a gig in New Orleans that I was going to talk to you about."

Wendy sighed and put down her fork. "Whew. I think I had too much wine."

"You know what? Let's get Pina to get some boxes and take the rest of this home. I'm gonna drive you home and we will get your car tomorrow."

Barry called Pina over for to-go boxes and the check. He reached into his coat pocket for his wallet, and pulled out an envelope that had been stuck inside.

"What's that, Dad?"

"Oh, I completely forgot to read this. It's from Grampy. He gave me this a couple of weeks ago." Barry opened it, read the first line and dropped the letter on the table.

"Oh my God."

"What is it, Dad? What does it say?"

Barry stared at the letter on the table. "Grammie's birthday is June 24th ."

"Duh … the same day as mine. This weekend." Wendy picked up the letter and read it aloud "What does it mean: 'I plan on getting Esther the birthday present she always wanted.'"

Barry picked up his cell phone and punched Dave Goldman's number. "DG … count me in. That's right. Save my spot. See ya, buddy."

"Wanna tell me what you are doing?"

"I am taking you to New Orleans for your birthday, honey."

SAMMY

DAY EIGHT

Better To Be Pissed Off
Than Pissed On

Audrey pulled up to the Shell Building and let Sammy out. One Shell Square is the largest office building in New Orleans and the home of Singerman Law Offices.

Charles Singerman occupied the 48th floor and was one of the most successful corporate lawyers in the state of Louisiana. He was also married to one of Esther and Sam's oldest friends, Rose Faye. Charlie was pushing 87 but still working fulltime and even though Rose Faye was having issues walking, she was always by his side.

When they were younger, they had often gone out on double dates with Sammy and Esther. Rose Faye had introduced Esther to Sammy when she was at Newcombe College. Sammy went to LSU in Baton Rouge but came home every weekend to work part time at Holtzman's, while Charlie was a Tulane Law School grad who caught Rose Faye's eye on their first date.

Over the years, they drifted apart as couples. They were in different social circles. Rose Faye and Charlie were naturally in the Lakefront group, while Sam and Esther were uptown Jews who gradually migrated to Metairie. But Sammy kept his Saints tickets with Charlie for a while before he moved to Florida. Esther played bridge with Rose Faye and the girls once a month.

It had been years since Sammy had seen or talked to Charlie, but today, that would change. He walked through the large glass front door, headed to the steel elevators and pressed the button marked 48.

Charlie would be waiting for him. Sammy had called for him while he was still living at Star of David. As the elevator climbed, Sammy thought about this meeting. There were always feelings of jealousy when Sammy was with Charlie. He was such a powerful wealthy man and Sammy always felt like the guy who had achieved so little in life. But today would be different. He didn't feel that way at all. In fact he looked forward to this meeting for a long time. Sammy bought a new suit and tie for the occasion. It wasn't as if he had any real business with Charlie but he just felt better dressing the part. Singerman hadn't even called him back. His secretary set up the meeting. Esther was in the backpack and all was right with the world.

Downstairs, Audrey parked in a visitor spot and waited for Sammy to return.

The elevator doors opened to an expansive lobby area that had large pieces of artwork on each wall. The Blue Dog looked down on Sammy. He stared at it for a minute or so. What the hell was that? A big blue dog with yellow eyes and a big daisy. Probably spent thousands of dollars for that piece of shit, he thought. On closer look, he saw the signature "Rodrigue" in the lower left corner. One lucky bastard, he bet. The facing wall held an abstract French Quarter scene from an artist named James Michalopoulos, according to the little title card mounted next to it. There were buildings squeezed into wavy shapes. Sammy laughed quietly and opened the glass door where Charles Singerman's office was housed.

Sammy looked around the office suite before he stepped up to the receptionist. "Morning," he finally said.

"Good morning sir," said the attractive woman who looked all of 21 and dressed to the nines. "What can I do for you?"

"Looking for Singerman. Um ... Charlie Singerman."

"And your name is?"

"Sam Levine."

She looked at her notes and picked up the phone. "Mr. Levine is here to see Mr. Singerman." She stood and motioned to the couch behind Sammy. "Please have a seat and Mr. Singerman's assistant will be out to get you shortly."

"Thanks." Sammy shuffled back to the couch. He chose one of the side chairs instead. The couch looked pretty comfortable, very plush and one that you could certainly sink right into. That's what Sammy was afraid of, he thought. Better take the solid chair that he could get up from easily.

The artwork inside was not as large as the outside pieces but equally impressive. There were a couple of Audubon prints of birds and a large painting of jazz musicians. In the corner was a sculpture of twisted trombones, trumpets, guitar and keyboards. A copy of New Orleans magazine sat prominently on the table in front of Sammy. It had a big picture of Charles Singerman on the cover. What a surprise, Sammy thought.

"Mr. Levine?" The voice startled Sammy, who was engrossed in thought.

"Yes?" He straightened his legs and slowly stood leaning on his cane.

"I am Elaine. Mr. Singerman's assistant." She shook his hand. "If you'll follow me. He is ready for you."

Sammy followed the efficient, bespectacled assistant down one hallway after another. Amazing, Sammy thought. Look at all these lawyers. They all busily worked behind windowed walls. He started to feel that old self consciousness whenever he was about to see Singerman ... even now that he was 86. He needed to shake this feeling. It's different this time. Elaine opened the door to the conference room. "Here you go Mr. Levine."

As soon as she opened the door, Singerman was right in front of him holding out a hand. "Sammy Levine! You old shit! How the hell are you?"

"Still a year younger than you, asshole." Sammy smiled immediately and shook his hand, put at ease by Singerman's greeting. As he entered the room, he saw Rose Faye leaning on one of the conference room chairs smiling. "Rose Faye? Is that you, dear?"

She came up to him and gave him a hug. "Hello Sammy. I am so happy you came to see us."

"I thought you might like to see Rosie. I told her to come along."

"Absolutely. How nice of you to come, Rose Faye. You look great."

Rose Faye patted his hand. "Oh you're such a good liar. Now Charles told me that you had some business to discuss with him today but I thought I would come see you too if that was okay?"

Sammy said, "Of course. I'm so glad you came."

"Let's all sit ... sit Sammy. Here, sit between Rose Faye and me." Singerman held a chair for Sammy to sit down. They both followed suit.

"We were so sorry to hear about Esther," Rose Faye said. "Must be very difficult without her."

Sammy reached in his backpack and took out the urn. "Oh, she is always with me. I know she's happy to see both of you."

Charlie and Rose Faye looked at each other for a second. "Well," Charlie finally said, "I'm glad she's ... with us today too."

"Sammy, what else brings you to New Orleans?" Rose Faye winked. "Aside from seeing us, of course."

Sammy took out the shoebox filled with mementos and opened his list. "Esther and I started to put together a bucket list of sorts, you know things that either she or I wanted to revisit or had planned to do but never did. Places, people, things that slipped by as time slipped by too. Esther passed before we were through and I have been living in independent living for a few years." Sammy looked down. "But one day I just said fuck it. Oh, sorry, Rose Faye."

"Silly boy. I still remember what that means." Rose Faye winked again.

"Well I just decided to break out and get this stuff done for both of us and bring her along with me."

Charlie laughed a hearty laugh. "That's terrific. So who's on it?"

"Well ... you and Rose Faye are. See?" He showed Charlie the list.

"We are honored."

Sammy pulled out the menu from the Sazerac. "We visited the Sazerac bar at the Roosevelt. Remember that one?"

Rose Faye chimed in. "Oh yes. Haven't gone in years. I remember when the four of us would get just plastered over there on our dates. Esther and I would get our Sazeracs and you boys would sip on your Old Fashioneds."

"Ha. I remember that well," Charlie added. "You used to always try to pick up the tab, Sammy."

"You remember that, Charlie?" Sammy asked.

"Sure. Rose Faye and I always used to say afterward that we wouldn't let you do that. Why, those bills probably were like a week's pay for you. Can't have you spend all your money. I had plenty even back then so ... I grabbed that sucker."

That old feeling of insecurity came back briefly. "Yes, you certainly did."

"So where did you go next?"

Sammy pulled out the book of matches. "Silk Stockings. It's a strip club. Never been to one. So I brought Esther there next."

"Oh my gosh!" Rose Faye giggled. "Always wanted to see what happens there myself!"

"It was really interesting." Sammy said. "And Chris Owens, remember her? She still dances there. She's older than we are." They all laughed. "You ever been to one, Charlie?" Sammy asked.

"Once or twice. We took clients there from time to time. Not really my cup of tea. But interesting. Very interesting."

Sammy took out the pinky ring. Singerman picked it up and look it over. "What's with the ring?"

"That's a 'gift' from Dickie Broussard. Remember Dickie Broussard?"

Rose Faye said. "I remember him. He was that bully at Fortier, I didn't think you two were friends."

"No, we weren't. Turns out that we went fishing on his son's boat. He ran the office so he and I kind of relived the old days a little before Tony, his son, cast off. It was a bucket list for Esther. She had never been fishing before. Dickie was an extra for me."

Sammy carefully took out the rest of the contents and placed them on the table. "So here's the remainder of our trip. Jazz Club that once was Holtzman's, my old furniture store. I got a piece of the building."

"Remember it well." Singerman said.

"A few stones from the Gates of Prayer Cemetery where my mom and dad and my son Michael are buried."

"I'm so sorry, Sammy," Rose Faye said.

"And finally, a bowling shirt from Mid City with my old employee Walter Smith's name embroidered. He owns Mid City now."

"Did a case for Walter," Charlie said.

"Well this is just wonderful, Sammy. I know you and Esther have shared some memories this week," Rose Faye said and looked at Charlie. "I know you two boys have business to discuss, too. So I am just going to step out and powder my nose."

Sammy reached over and gave Rose Faye a hug. "It was wonderful to see you."

"And you too, Sammy. If you are in town for a while we would love to have you over for dinner."

"Maybe another time. This is a short trip. But it is most gracious of you to ask," Sammy said.

"I'll meet you at home, Charles." Rose Faye said as she left.

"Yes, dear." Charlie said.

Singerman looked at his watch one more time. He pushed a button on the conference phone. "Elaine, I will be with Mr. Levine for a little while longer. Please tell the mayor I'll be with him momentarily."

"The mayor? Wow. I am really honored that you are giving me some of his time. I know how busy you are, Charlie. I'll make it quick."

"Not a problem." Charlie sat down and folded his hands. "Sammy, would you like a memento from Rose Faye and me? He reached in his coat pocket. "A pen from the law firm, or … ?"

Before Charlie could finish, Sammy interrupted. "No, thank you. I wouldn't think of it. Besides …" He pushed all the mementos in front of Charlie. "These are all for you, Mr. Singerman."

"Sammy, these are yours. Why would you give them to me?"

"Because my dear friend, they belong to you, too."

Sammy walked around the table to face Singerman. "You see, Esther always had such a fondness for you so we both thought that we would find and share mementos that had special meaning for you as well."

"I don't understand."

"You will." He leaned on his cane. His back was aching but he didn't want to stop. "Esther's fondness went well beyond just admiration. I remember hearing the words, 'Why can't you be like Charlie Singerman? Why can't you be rich like Charlie Singerman? Why can't you look like Charlie Singerman?'" His voice got louder as he went further.

"Sam, I'm sorry that she felt that way. But surely you can't blame me for that."

"Wrong! I can blame you … CHARLIE!" He picked up the Sazerac menu. "Esther used to frequent the Sazerac Bar without me at times. I know this because — and I'm not proud of this — I followed her. And guess who also happened to frequent the Sazerac Bar on those nights?"

Charlie stood. "Now, just a minute. What are you saying?"

Sammy continued, "I'm saying that you and Esther would meet at the Roosevelt, have a drink or two at the bar and then get a room." He picked up the matches. "And the Strip Club? Another hangout for you and Esther. I guess you felt safe there because you wouldn't be recognized. Or if you were, nobody would admit being there, either." Sammy reached in his backpack for a folder filled with receipts and tax bills. "Oh, wait a minute. They just might recognize you because I forgot to add that you are a silent partner in Silk Stocking."

Singerman stood angrily. "Get out, Sammy. This has gone far enough."

"Not yet. Not nearly far enough. You were also Sam Holtzman's attorney. YOU drafted the paperwork that put me in charge of the store without any compensation and left me with all the liability when he took all the assets and left me holding the bag. I know he shared the wealth with you. You were in on it all the time."

"You're crazy. Sam Holtzman was a greedy son of a bitch and you were a gullible patsy. Not my fault he died and left you holding the bag."

"Not your fault he died, but I know you profited." He held up Walter's shirt. "Walter knew the details because he heard you and Sam in your office planning it. If I could prove it, I would have you put in jail."

"You are swimming in dangerous waters, Sam, with these unfounded allegations."

"Unfounded, my ass. You are a crook and a cheat. Dickie Broussard? You know Dickie, don't you Charlie?" He held up the ring. "You continue to defend that asshole even though he is a known drug lord and scumbag. Does he treat you well? Huh?"

Singerman punched the number on the phone and Sammy ripped it out of his hands.

"Sit down, Charlie. I'm almost done here. Listen, I'm no angel. I had an affair and I wasn't proud of it. Esther was unhappy and I drifted. I'm not defending myself on that." Sammy pointed at the urn. "But you strung this woman along and took advantage of her feelings for you for three years. You told her you loved her and that you were going to marry her and kept filling her head with bullshit promises."

"I am NOT going to sit here and listen to you blame me for your unhappiness after all these years. Lies! These are all lies."

Sammy dug into his knapsack and pulled out pictures and letters and threw them at Singerman. "I'm lying? Look at these. Pictures of you both at the strip club and the Roosevelt. Recognize them? And letters you sent. I've held on to these for years. Esther kept them hidden and I found them after she died. Proof, Charlie. Proof." He lowered his voice and leaned on the table. "Esther was devastated when you broke it off. She changed after that. Her mind snapped and she was never the same. We couldn't go out, she was afraid of everything ... flying, crowded rooms, elevators. When Mikey died, she tried to kill herself, too. I found her in the bathroom ..." He loosened his tie. "You were always a self-centered piece of shit. You really got off on your self-importance, made me feel small because I didn't have the wealth or the friends or the standing that you did."

Singerman hung his head and slumped in his chair. He looked suddenly very old and very fragile as he looked at pictures of them embracing in a corner of the strip club under low light and another checking in to the Roosevelt and another in his car.

Sammy continued: "You can keep those. I have taken the liberty to duplicate them and have copies of your love/hate letters as well. You can keep the strip club paperwork, too. One set I thought of sending to the paper and the other set to Rose Faye. Maybe the mayor would want to see a copy, huh? Should we call him in?" Sammy started go for the door.

"No!" Singerman stood. "You wouldn't dare. Rose Faye ... it would kill her. Why would you do that?"

"Excuse me? Why would I do that? A better question would be: Why did YOU do that, Charlie? I'm sure there were others. Rose Faye probably knows you're a slime ball. What do you think? And the newspaper? Nobody really cares and nobody reads them anymore, huh Charlie?"

Singerman slumped again and reached in his jacket. "What do you want Sammy? Money? How much?" He pulled out his checkbook and started writing.

"You think you can buy me off? Like a cash settlement, in your lawyer jargon. Like pain and suffering and, let's see, doctor's bills and hospitalizations?" Sammy stared at

Singerman with a look of total dominance. He let time pass for the dramatic effect. "Okay, Charles … How about $250,000."

Singerman breathed a heavy sigh. "You will destroy the letters and the pictures?"

"Sure."

Singerman paused. "You want this in your name?"

"No. Make the check out to Barry Levine." Sammy dug his hand into his empty pants pocket. "And can you also give me whatever cash you have on you, too? I'm a little short."

Singerman handed Sammy the check and counted out $1,655 that he pulled out of his pocket. Sammy grabbed the check, the money and his knapsack, putting Esther gently back inside. "Esther and I really enjoyed getting together with you Charles. And it was a real pleasure doing business with you."

He turned and pushed the door open and walked straight out to the elevators.

Suddenly, he stopped. He wanted to do one more thing before he left. He faced the Blue Dog, unzipped his fly and relieved himself.

All the while Sammy was singing, "Don't it make your blue dog, don't it make your blue dog, don't it make your blue dog … GREEN."

DAY NINE

Let It Ride

"Remind me again why we are here?" Audrey held onto Sammy's arm as they pushed open the large doors at Harrah's Casino and stepped through the velvet ropes at the security desk.

"This, my dear, is Esther's favorite place in the world."

"Esther was a gambler?"

Sammy let out his hoarse shoulder-shaking chuckle and said, "Not just 'a' gambler, more like 'a crazy, get your hands off my machine or I'll break your face' gambler. She spent hours here. Also, spent almost all our money, many times over."

"I have seen more than a few Esthers here," said Audrey. "Sounds like you had your hands full."

Sammy took Esther out of the knapsack as he paused and slowly turned around with her urn tightly at his chest. "Okay, Miss Esther. Where would you like to go first?"

"If she says 'the bathroom,' I'll lead the way," Audrey said as she pointed to the restroom signs. "Gotta pee, Sam."

"Okay. We're gonna be in the high limit slots. Her favorite machine is the Triple Diamonds."

Audrey made a beeline to the left and Sammy shuffled off to the right.

As they walked he talked softly to Esther. "There's the buffet, honey. I remember they had the softest rolls. Remember that? And the desserts. You loved those desserts. The bananas foster, the carrot cake, the pies. Getting hungry just thinking about it. Oh, I know, I know, you want to get to your machine. I'm not stopping ..."

An older woman patted Sammy on the arm as she walked next to him. "Excuse me. Is that an urn?"

Sammy turned to look at her. "It sure would be an ugly a flower pot now, wouldn't it?"

She was wearing a white Harrah's sweatshirt with lots of glitter around the logo. It was 90 degrees outside but apparently she was still cold. "I couldn't help but overhear your conversation. Your wife?"

"Yes."

"How sweet. You must miss talking to her."

Sammy stopped and rested for a second. "Truth is, I never got a word in when she was alive. So I'm making up for lost time."

"My husband passed last year. He and I would talk for hours." She looked at the urn. "I miss him dearly. I just visited him at Sacred Heart Cemetery." She looked around and then whispered. "I still talk to him."

Sammy shook his head and stood for another few seconds and finally said. "Well, we have some gambling to do. Gotta go."

"Try the Poker Joker in the back corner. Harvey told me that it's been hot tonight."

"Harvey's your husband?"

She laughed. "Oh, heavens no. Harvey is the cashier in the high limit room." Sammy nodded and started to turn. She continued. "My husband told me that the 7's were gonna pay out but I never listen to him."

Sammy sat Esther's urn on the Triple Diamonds player's chair and put a hundred dollar bill in the slot. "Compliments of your old boyfriend, Miss Esther."

He pushed MAX BET and watched the bars and the cherries and the symbols spin wildly on the $5 machine. When Esther was alive he would have never pushed MAX BET on any machine much less a $5 one. Esther always gambled in High Limit, while Sammy wandered the casino looking for the Penny Slots. He was not a gambler and had a sick feeling in his stomach every time she gambled. He insisted going with her each time she visited. If he didn't, they might have never gotten out of the poorhouse. Many of their trips ended in major blowups, name-calling and the ever-present "Why can't you be more like Charlie Singerman?" remarks followed by "I should have married him." Well, he thought, Charlie Singerman can kiss my ass. But first, he can pay the price for their sins. Sin tax, that's what this is. Sin tax.

Each MAX BET spin was $15 on the Triple Diamonds machine and Sammy noticed that he was down to $30 as he hit the button. "Let's get a jackpot Esther and really show Charlie Singerman that we are big players."

Nothing.

Audrey came up behind Sammy's chair just about that time. "Too bad, Esther," she said. "There's still $15 left."

"Hit the button, Strippergirl. You might be the lucky one today."

"I am never lucky, Sammy. You sure?"

"Hit it."

The wheels spun and the first one showed the triple diamond logo. "That's it, baby." Sammy said. The second wheel landed on a trip diamond too. Now there was a duet of "Holy shit!" from Audrey and Sammy. Then the third wheel hit and there it was.

Jackpot!

The machine lit up. BIG WIN registered on its face. Jackpot music played and Sammy and Audrey jumped for joy. They almost knocked Esther off the chair in their excitement over winning $5,000.

Suddenly Audrey stopped. "Wait, Sammy." She picked up Esther and handed her to Sammy. Then she slipped into the players chair herself.

"Jackpot payouts come with a tax form and they always ask for identification. I'll give them mine."

"Are you sure?"

Audrey shooed him away. "Go play another one. I'll find you." He didn't move. "Oh. You don't trust me, huh? You think I'm going to run off with your $5,000? Is that what you think?"

Sammy just smiled. "No. I was just going to say thanks. For taking such good care of me."

Audrey noticed the slot attendant coming closer. "Go. Get out of here you old bastard."

"Slut!" Sammy said as he turned, still smiling.

As he walked to the other side of the High Limit room, he eyed a familiar sparkly sweatshirt. It was the woman he ran into earlier and she was playing Joker Poker on the far wall.

"So, did it hit yet?" He asked.

She looked up surprised. "Oh hi. No. I think Harvey must have been had a little too much to drink tonight." She made a drunk face and shrugged. "How'd you do?"

"We hit a jackpot — $5,000."

"Hey. That's great." She held out her hand to shake it. "I'm Clarice by the way."

"Sammy," he said and shook her hand. "This is Esther, my wife."

"Esther, huh? Are you from New Orleans?"

"Lived here our whole lives until we moved to Florida a while back."

She scratched her head and said. "Funny. There was a gal that came here a lot and played here in the High Limits. We used to talk about life and marriage and stuff. Her name was Esther, too." She laughed. "Her husband hated to gamble and would have really hit the roof if he knew how often she came here when he didn't know …" She stopped short and looked at Sammy's face."

"Oh shit."

"Couldn't have said it better myself."

"I am so sorry." She pointed to the urn. "This is THAT Esther, and you are …"

"The schmuck that hated when she gambled. It's okay. It wasn't a secret." He looked down at the urn. "I'm actually happy to meet someone who knew her."

Clarice said, "I wouldn't say that I really knew her that well. But you know how women are. We yak a lot when we are together and spill our guts."

"So what did you two talk about?"

"Well, I know you have two sons right?"

Sammy nodded.

"And your youngest passed away from cancer. Very sad." She patted his hand. "She told me how hard that was but how lucky she was to have her oldest son and how wonderful he was with his brother."

"Very true."

"And she talked a lot about you."

He sat up straight. "That's okay. Maybe we better stop here."

"You both were very different and you fought a lot. But through it all, she loved you very much." Clarice kept holding his hand. "She said that she had made lots of mistakes. She didn't elaborate on those, but she did say that you were the most understanding man she ever met." Clarice sat back. "Who doesn't fight? My husband was so hard-headed. We fought constantly. I always loved him, too. But anyway, Esther said that even through the fighting and name calling, you were always there for her."

"She ... She really said all that?"

"She did."

Audrey appeared. "Okay. All cashed out."

Clarice looked up. "Who is this lovely young lady?"

Sammy piped up. "Audrey. She's a stripper." He started to say more but Audrey grabbed Sam by the hand.

"Nice to meet you Audrey. I'm Clarice." she said.

"It was a pleasure meeting you, too. I have to get Sammy back to the asylum before they lock him out."

Clarice laughed and Sammy bent down to kiss her cheek. "Thanks for being a friend to Esther."

He turned and looked at Clarice as they were leaving. "And to me, too."

"She said that Esther loved me very much," Sammy said as he collapsed into the living room chair in Audrey's apartment. "How do you like that?"

"Well, duh!" Audrey answered. "Of course, she loved you. Did you think she didn't?"

Sammy took off his cap and laid it on the table. "I thought it was always Charlie Singerman."

"Not a chance. He was her escape from reality when things got too hard. She didn't really love him. She just wanted to make life shitty for you because she felt life was shitty for her."

"Well, doctor, thanks for your diagnosis."

Audrey sat on the table in front of Sam. "Sammy, you told me that Esther had some issues. I'm sure you did, too. Everybody does. But she had some serious shit going on like her shopping binges and her depression and her gambling. She was a really smart lady who never used her brain for anything useful. Right? She didn't work until you guys were much older. She didn't want kids but she had two, she resented her friends with money."

"She sounds like a real bitch."

Sammy smiled.

"She probably was. But that hasn't stopped you from taking her ashes all over the city, talking to her night and day, and protecting her even though she's not breathing any more." Audrey squeezed his skinny shoulders. "She is very lucky to have had you. I can see how much you loved her and in her own way, I know she loved you too."

They sat for a long time Sammy's eyes filled with tears as he looked at Audrey in all her stripper girl splendor. Actually, without the heavy makeup and the 10 inch heels, she looked like a little girl. She was very pretty, Sammy thought. Also, pretty damned smart. There was that far off look of sadness in her, too. It made her appear even younger and more vulnerable.

Hah! Vulnerable she wasn't. She's the first person to take with you to a knife fight. God help the opponent. But still, there was sadness. Only natural when you think about her life, her childhood, all that she'd endured.

He had grown so attached to Audrey.

She didn't know it yet but she was also one of the people on his bucket list. He would tell her more about that tomorrow, right after Esther's birthday surprise. And right before he went back home.

"Sammy? Are you okay?" Audrey asked.

He wiped his eyes. "Yeah, I'm fine. Lots of pollen or dust in here. You need to clean this place up."

"Well I got this old guy staying with me who is a pig. Leaves his dirty underwear and socks all over the place and never cleans up the bathroom."

"You should kick his ass out."

"I might just do that. I can't afford to take care of that old fart anymore."

Sammy put his hand on hers. "I heard tomorrow is his last day."

Audrey stared into his eyes. "It is?"

"Yes, my dear. Tomorrow we will celebrate Esther's birthday and then I'm done. Time to get back to Florida."

Audrey stood up quickly and began straightening up the living room, fluffing pillows and brushing off imaginary lint. "Well, it's about time. I gotta get back to work and pay bills."

Sammy grabbed her hand as she brushed by. "Hey, sit down for a minute. I want to ask you something."

Audrey sat.

"The stripping thing. I was wondering ..."

"Why a girl like me does it? Or what will I do with my life after my body goes to shit? Or how could I have been so stupid to do this in the first place?" Audrey's voice was rising.

"You're not stupid."

"What is it with men? They all ask the same damned thing."

"So? I want to know. Why do you do it?"

Audrey answered like an airhead would: "Um ... like it pays WELL, you know? I mean I make a lot of money just to move my ass and let guys touch me a little. Where else can I get easy money like that ... you know?"

"Sorry."

Audrey sat and tried to calm down. "Look, it's a decent living. I know I can get something else. Something better, maybe. Not necessarily that pays as well 'cause I haven't been to school. Maybe one day, I don't know."

"So what would you do if stripping wasn't an option?"

"Um, massage therapy, maybe?"

"Bullshit." Sammy said.

"Why? You don't think I would be good at it?"

"I don't think you want to be a massage therapist. Sounds like another stripper answer."

Audrey got up walked into her bedroom. She came back with a stack of books and dropped them on the table. Sammy picked them up and looked at the covers: Mechanical Engineering Basics, Car Mechanics for the New Age, Top Inventions of the Modern Era.

"Engineering?"

"I wanna build something … invent something." Audrey picked up the books. "Okay, sure. Have a laugh on me. The stripper who designs mechanical sex toys or something. That's what people would think. No one would believe that I have a brain and an interest in engineering. That's why I never tell anybody what I really want to be when I grow up."

"Of course, you have a brain. A big one. I think that's incredible. Why don't you do it? What's stopping you?"

"Well let's see. For one thing, about $100,000 to get an engineering degree, And let's see another thing is $100,000 for an engineering degree. Oh and there's $100,000 for an engineering degree."

"There are other jobs."

Audrey stopped the conversation and pivoted. "Enough about me. Let's see the plans for tomorrow before you bail on me."

Sammy reached in his pocket and pulled out his little pieces of paper outlining the plans for the morning. Audrey read each one as Sammy looked at her face.

"Very cool! She will love it. We need to invite everybody we can think of. Sally and the Ballers, Walter, everybody. This will be a huge celebration for Esther."

"Audrey," Sammy said as he put his arm around her. "I know you don't trust many people because so many have bailed on you. I just want you to know, tomorrow even though I'm going home, I'll never bail on you."

Audrey smiled. "I know."

DAY TEN

Sleeping With The Lakefront Jews

"**B**e careful with that cake." Sammy scolded Sally as she almost tripped on a piece of loose carpeting in front of the baked goods department at Walmart.

Sally flipped him off as she gently placed the cake in Sammy's cart. Through the clear plastic cover, Sammy checked the finished product. On the top of the chocolate frosting sat a tiny urn sitting at one end of a rainbow made from colored frosting. At the other end was a dolphin jumping out of the cake. The message in pink read: "Happy Birthday and Smooth Sailing Miss Esther."

"Perfect. She will love it." Sammy said as he patted the knapsack where Esther was under wraps. "Now where is Audrey?"

"She's in the party section, picking out some balloons and other party shit, I think," Sally answered as she checked her makeup in the freezer sliding glass door.

"I'll check on her." Sammy shuffled off to the area that held all the party items. He passed the section with chips and pretzels, picking through the snacks and dumping them in his cart. He took out the notes that Audrey had given him for Walmart shopping and randomly made mental check marks of things he had finished. He was great at planning Esther's party but pretty bad at planning the menu details. Audrey, it turned out, was good at that.

He turned into the party aisle as Audrey was trying on party hats and crazy glasses with birthday messages around the rims. "Hey, look at all this great stuff," She motioned to Sammy. "Streamers and big balloons and sparklers. Can we get them?"

"Sure thing. Pile them in." Even though Ira and Arthur and Sandy's credit cards were still in his wallet, Sammy didn't want to take a chance at this point of drawing suspicion or worse being arrested if they have finally been frozen. Thankfully, he still had the cash left from Charlie Singerman's shakedown and there was plenty of cash from the casino win even after he split it with Audrey. "Aw, what the hell. Let's get the big speakers we passed out front and that music karaoke machine, too."

What a sight they were tooling down Lakeshore Drive in the red mustang with the top down, balloons bouncing around and radio blaring. Audrey was at the wheel, Sally was in shotgun and Sammy was in back. Behind them was a carload of strippers and customers from Silk Stockings. They borrowed the Silk Stocking club bus.

"Okay, slow down a little up ahead," Sammy said. "I think the place is up here to the left." They passed big residential houses partially hidden by the levees that protected them. Sammy looked for the landmark that marked the spot.

"There! That's it. The big white lighthouse up ahead. Go past it and there is a shelter and a big parking lot right on the water." Sure enough, the shelter was there and no one had claimed it. It was one of many shelters scattered all along Lakeshore Drive and they were all public and free to use, first come, first served. After Katrina, many were destroyed but they were built back and much of Lakeshore Drive (including the Lighthouse) was restored and even enhanced.

Sally pulled in facing the water and Sammy stepped out onto the grass for the first time in twenty years. "Esther and I came here all the time. Shelter No. 1. Her favorite spot. We'd pack a lunch and sit on the levee steps watching the waves." He pointed behind him. "Back there is where the rich Jews lived."

The Silk Stocking bus pulled up and unloaded the masses and they carried bags of food, party favors, ice chests filled with beer, card tables, folding chairs, strands of lights, the sound system ... and within a matter of minutes the party was in full swing.

S ammy leaned on his cane in a folding chair that sat next to the large picnic table where he had placed Esther's urn. The urn sported a party hat, Mardi Gras beads and a big pair of sunglasses. Next to the urn was a framed picture of Sammy and Esther in their younger days. Esther had a New Year's Eve party hat with 1970 written in glitter, beads and a big pair of sunglasses that became her trademark. Sam had a flowered shirt, beads, giant glasses that were at least as big as Esther's and a big smile on his face. Mikey was on one side and Barry was on the other. Each boy had noisemakers and blew them at the same time the picture was taken. "Miss Esther, Happy Birthday. I know you're smiling. This is your party. I hope you like it. I figured this is how you'd want to celebrate and just where you want to be."

"Pretty cool party, old man." Mercedes said as she and Sally and Audrey walked over and sat on the ground next to Sammy. She handed him a beer.

"Are you happy?" Audrey asked.

"Very." Sammy said.

"Hey, I was asking Esther." Audrey playfully punched him in the arm.

"She's not saying much. Kinda taking it in."

They all three hugged him and kissed him on the cheek and scattered into the crowd dancing and singing Leslie Gore's It's My Party, one of the many songs in the mix that DJ Norm put together at the club for the party today. Next up was Live and Let Die followed by Wake Me Up Before You Go Go, Frank Sinatra's I'm Gonna Live Until I Die, Dead Man's Party by Oingo Boingo and of course Billy Joel's Only the Good Die Young. There's one he will save until the end of the day depending on Sammy's mood ... the saddest anthem of lost love, Tears In Heaven.

This is Esther's day, Sammy thought to himself as he looked around at the neighborhood. He wasn't really a big fan of the Lakefront. He knew she was and he knew why. Singerman lived right down the street. For a moment he thought about trashing the house with the help of all his new friends but he already had his revenge. Anything else would be just anticlimactic. Besides, that would only upset Rose Faye. Sammy never wanted her to be affected by his Singerman attack. She was so sweet and loving to everyone. Too bad she picked that schmuck as a husband.

Sammy had a lot of time for soul searching on this journey. He was pretty miserable the last few years, maybe the last few decades. Was he every bit as much of a schmuck as Charlie? His unhappiness seemed to keep people away from him lately. Surely he had a good reason, he thought. The food sucked at Star of David, he was 86 years old for God's sake and close to the end. He felt like shit every day. The doctors told him that his heart could give out at any moment (a fact he didn't even broach with Dr. Trestman). And he didn't have any friends except for old Stan, who didn't talk.

Michael was gone. Thank heavens he still had Barry. He was a good son. Better than Sammy deserved, that's for sure. Smart boy ... and talented. Audrey was right. Mikey was Sammy's favorite because he could talk to him about the business and because he was more like Sammy. What a self-centered bastard he was. Then Mikey went and died on him. So what did Sammy do? Ignored Barry even more. Like it was his fault that he was now his only son, the son who didn't connect with his father. Barry was always nagging him about ... about ... taking better care of himself.

"Hah! What an asshole, I am," Sammy thought. "I get short with Barry because he nags me about taking better care of myself. He is always there for me whenever I need anything and he listens to me bitch about everything in the world."

"Mr. Sam!" Walter Smith plopped down a huge platter of ribs, wings and crawfish. "You hungry?"

"Well if it isn't my favorite ..."

"Schvartze?" Walter asked.

"No." Sammy said as he stood to give Walter a hug. "I was going to say billionaire bowler." He hugged him tightly. "Besides, LeBron is my favorite schvartze."

"Hah! Dare you to tell HIM that."

"Not a chance." He smiled at Walter. "Thanks, Walter."

"For what?"

"For everything."

Just then it seemed like the entire party descended on Walter and the delicious food he just put on the tables. Caesar from Sazerac came by to help with drinks and Esther's sweet little friend from the casino pulled up in a big Cadillac with a few of her gambling cronies.

"Look, girls, there's Esther on the table. Remember those big sunglasses?" They all burst into laughter and bustled over to Sammy to introduce themselves. There was Bertha Melancon in a big bright sundress; Cheryl Trapani, who stood at 4-feet-10 even in platform heels, and Pat Guidry, who at six feet tall seemed like she was 6-feet-10 next to Cheryl. They all shared funny Esther stories for the crowd and Sam in particular.

Sammy was happy. It was a word he wouldn't have even attempted to use to describe himself — in, well — he couldn't remember when the last time was that he felt happy or even content.

Audrey came to him. It was as if she could read his mind. "Well, you look pretty pleased with yourself, Mr. Sam."

He knew it was time to tell her. He felt a sense of anxiousness. He had waited long enough. "Audrey, there is something I need to tell you."

"Sure, what's up?"

"Let's go over to the water, away from the noise. Can you bring us a couple of chairs?"

"Well now you're scaring me. This sounds serious," she said as she picked up two folding chairs and carried them down to the lip of the levee. Sammy grabbed his and opened it up facing her. "Are you pregnant?" Audrey asked.

"Twins," Sammy said with a twinkle in his eyes. "Don't worry. I'll raise them alone. You don't need to send me any support payments." They both laughed. "Seriously, I have been meaning to tell you this from the first time we met." He opened a manila envelope he pulled from his knapsack and took out a photo and handed it to her.

She looked at it. It was an older picture, yellowed with time and it showed a young woman posing with a couple in front of a pawn shop. Audrey studied it. "Who are they?"

"Well, the guy on the left is my older brother, Ben, and he is standing next to his wife Jeanette in front of their pawn shop in Indianapolis."

Audrey pointed to the younger woman standing to the right. "And that girl kinda looks like me."

"It does looks like you. Probably because it's your grandmother, Audrey."

"No way. My grandmother knew your brother?"

"She worked for him. Until your mother was born, that is." Sammy studied Audrey's face. "Sadly, she died in childbirth."

"What was her name?"

"Her name was Lorraine. Lorraine Gallagher," Sam continued. "My brother Ben and his wife took in Rosie after Lorraine died and raised her. They had no children, so they were thrilled to have Rosie."

"Are you saying that my mother was raised by your brother?" Audrey stared in disbelief.

"She never talked about any of this. As far as I knew, I had no grandparents at all. They were all dead and I never knew."

"I think Ben and Jeanette were probably 'dead to her,' from what Benny told me later. Your mom was kind of a wild child. She carried the same genetic trait that killed your grandmother and that caused her to live life in full gear, I guess. Not knowing what the future would hold. She left home as a teenager after a series of arguments over how she lived her life. Nobody was going to tell her what to do. Benny tried to get her back home but failed and eventually, they lost touch completely."

Audrey got very silent. She was balancing many mixed emotions. She was elated that she was finally getting some closure on her family members — this was what she always dreamed about. But she felt oddly uneasy about Sammy knowing all this information and not sharing earlier. Or just even knowing. How did he know so much? Audrey never talked about this to anyone. She didn't want to be treated any differently. She also hated to face the grim reality about her genetic makeup. She knew that Huntington's Disease was hereditary. There's a 50 percent chance that she could have it. The brutal death of her mother and the agony that she endured during the latter stages haunted her constantly.

"Audrey," Sammy continued, "I understand why you feel ..."

"Like a freak? Is that what you're trying to say? Or are you going to say 'why I feel like I'm just going to have to be a stripper because I don't have a future? Oh sure I know about Huntington's. I've read all the books. I know what my future is." She stood over him. "And what was that bullshit conversation we had about what I'm going to do with my life?

Were you just trying to find out what the DYING GIRL wants to do?"

"Audrey!"

"And why do you care ANYWAY?"

"Because I'm your grandfather, that's why."

Audrey stood as if hit by a bolt of lightning and then sat. "Oh, my God," she exclaimed, trying to piece the puzzle in her head.

"Lorraine was the girl I fell in love with the day she walked into Holtzman's." He embarrassedly looked down at the water, not making eye contact. "When I had to let her go, I asked Benny if he could find a spot for her. He did. I didn't know she was pregnant. Benny called me months later to tell me when she was already in the throes of her disease. She was so sick. I called all the time and she never wanted to talk to me. Benny told me that she was going it alone. She did not want to destroy my marriage." He laughed a short evil kind of laugh. "Destroy my marriage! That's a joke. Charlie Singerman was helping that one along just fine."

Audrey turned away. She couldn't look at Sammy. She was angry. This was my grandfather? He never came to find us all these years?

"Rosie looked to be the picture of health when she was growing up. I visited her often and Benny and Jeanette came to New Orleans regularly. I sent them money to help with expenses but they kept sending it back."

"Getting close to sundown," Audrey said. "Probably should get to the second part of the celebration, huh?"

"Almost done. So, things went south when Rosie was 13. Benny tried to protect her. She stole money from the register, tried to sell some of the pawn items to some questionable friends and got involved with drugs. She got arrested twice before she was 14 for stealing a car and robbing a 7-11 with the same circle of friends."

"Yeah, my mom was bad … blah blah blah."

"Audrey, your mom was your mom. She's not you. I lost your grandmother, I lost your mom and I lost you." He hugged her. "When she left my brother's house, no one could find her. It took me years to find you. I didn't even know you existed until a friend of your mom's came in to the Pawn Shop a few years ago."

She was crying with her hands frozen to her sides.

"Benny told me where your last address was and I traced you to New Orleans. That's one of the main reason I'm here. YOU AND ESTHER are my bucket list."

Audrey wiped her face and managed a small smile. Her head was spinning but she had really formed a special connection with this old bastard with the funky backpack and the crooked body. "Okay, Sammy. Let's celebrate your other woman!"

The sun was setting. DJ Norm quieted the crowd and gave Sammy a karaoke mic to begin. " Thank you … thank you very much. I just wanted to tell all of you what a special day …"

"GRAMPY!" Sammy stopped and squinted his eyes to shut out the setting sun and to get a better look at the figure sprinting toward him. There were other figures following behind.

"Wendy?" Sammy said, barely holding it together.

She ran into his arms and hugged him and kissed him. "We knew. We knew where you'd be. Daddy read your note. I missed you, Grampy."

"I missed you, too, honey. I am so glad you're here."

Barry stood back and managed a little wave. "Hi, Dad." He took a cap out of his back pocket and handed it to Sammy. It read: "Throw me something, Mister!"

Sammy proudly put it on. He stood there holding back tears when he saw Barry. He wanted to hug him but chose to wave as well and say, "Thanks, son." Barry nodded. Suddenly Sammy grabbed Barry's hand. "Fuck it." He pulled Barry to him and gave him an enormous hug. Karen rushed in and put her arms around both of them. "Hi, Dad!" She also hugged him tight.

"You still hanging around with this guy?"

"Only on days that include you."

"Is that David? And Tony? And Mickey? And Pinchus? The whole band huh?"

"Yes sir." Dave piped in. "Hope it's okay."

Sammy picked up the mic and blew into it. "Hey everybody. This is my family. My granddaughter Wendy, my daughter-in-law ... I still consider her my daughter-in-law ... Karen, my son's band and my ... my son." He broke up for a minute, choking back tears. "My terrific boy, Barry." Barry teared up also, not expecting that. "They are all here just like you are here today, my new friends." He looked around and then pointed at a fat guy chewing on a rib not paying any attention. "Like that guy, whoever he is, to celebrate Esther's birthday and ... hey, listen it's Wendy's birthday, too. So first off can you join me in singing happy birthday?"

All broke into a disjointed version with the line ... Happy Birthday Esther and Wendy ... and ended with a big round of applause.

Sammy resumes. "That was great. And next ... we want to wish her a safe journey as we say good bye as well. This is Esther's final resting spot. The place she always wanted to live when she was alive and now the next best thing. The place she will remain for eternity. I want to thank all of you for making Esther and me feel welcome. Especially Audrey." Audrey ducked down. "Or Destiny as many of you might know her. Forget I said her real name." Lots of chuckles from the crowd as Sammy winked. "And all the people at Silk Stockings for coming out and setting stuff up." The Silk Stockings gang wildly applauded.

Sammy sat gingerly, still holding the microphone. "I hope you don't mind if I sit to say the rest. I'm feeling a little tired." He had beads of sweat on his forehead and upper lip. "Before we end I just wanted to tell you a little about Esther. To those who didn't know he, she was a real force of nature. She was strong-willed, very bright and unwilling to accept mediocrity. And to those who knew her ..." He stopped to look at the family. "Well, she was a real bitch."

Gasps and then laughter erupted. "It's true, you know it. But she was also very thoughtful and very caring in her own way. She loved every one of her 400 pairs of shoes and 2,000 dresses that she couldn't afford. And although she said many times that she never wanted kids, she loved both her sons very much." He stopped momentarily to wipe his eyes. "Wendy, come up here." Wendy scooted in beside him. "She really loved her granddaughter the most. Wendy, would you and the girls help me hand out roses to all the guests?"

Wendy came to her Grampy's side. Audrey and the other girls carried dozens of roses and handed them to the guests one by one.

"DJ Norm, would you play Esther's favorite Frank Sinatra tune please?"

Sammy lifted Esther into his arms as Wendy steadied him on the other side. They walked to the levee and the crowd followed forming a semicircle around the edges. Sammy stepped down three steps and held onto Wendy's arm. Barry stood close by behind the couple to make sure all was steady. The sound of My Way now filled the air and roses were held aloft on either side of Sammy.

He smiled and kissed the urn. "Wendy, would you open the top for me?"

"You did it your way, Miss Esther."

He scattered the ashes into Lake Pontchartrain, with a little help from the family and as he signaled the crowd, all threw their roses in the water. It was a beautiful sight, Sammy thought. Just like he imagined it would be. The song faded and all stood in silence for a few minutes as the sounds of the waves gently came in and the sky darkened gradually.

One last act, Sammy thought to himself.

A s Sammy sat comfortably in a folding chair with Wendy by his side, Audrey came over and bent down to whisper in his ear, "Asshole."

"I love you too, strippergirl."

She gently kissed the side of his face.

Sammy stood quickly. "Okay, okay ... there is one more thing that would make our trip complete. Barry and Wendy?

Do you have guitars with you?"

Dave stood up. I've got two in the car."

"Good. Because there is a special request that I have …" Sammy began coughing. He was pale and drawn. Tired, he thought. Really tired.

"Are you okay, dad?" Barry asked.

"Fine … just fine. Son, sit here next to me and Wendy sit on the other side. Barry, would you and Wendy sing the song you wrote for her when she was just a toddler. It was Esther's favorite of all your songs. And mine too."

Barry and Wendy sang in perfect harmony:

Propped up on pillows
Under the sheets
She looks up at me and she smiles.

Tell me a story dad
Sing me to sleep
Stay with me here for a while.

Daddy take me to the circus
Daddy take me there tonight
Daddy please make me a princess

DADDY DON'T TURN OUT THE LIGHT.

Sometimes she listens politely
As I read to her from a book
And sometimes we lie down together
Reliving adventures we took.

Maybe one day we'll grow wings and we'll fly
Stare into space and count stars in the sky.
We will fight dragons and rescue the queen
It's the magic of living a dream.

Propped up on pillows
Under the sheets
He looks up at me and he smiles.
Tell me a story Dad
Sing me to sleep
Stay with me here for a while.

Daddy take me to the circus
Daddy take me there tonight
Daddy please make me a princess
DADDY DON'T TURN OUT THE LIGHT.

There was not a dry eye in the park. There was applause and tears. Barry looked around and there were girls hugging each other saying things like "I wish my Daddy had written a song like that for me." The beer drinkers were still chugging and his band members bowed in unison at his greatness.

Barry looked down at Sammy. His hand rested on Barry's leg. His eyes were closed and his breathing had stopped. He looked peaceful and content and once and for all …

… happy.

The End

SAMMY

EPILOGUE

Paying It Forward

Audrey couldn't make a decision. She flipped through the TV stations like she was possessed. None of the shows sounded interesting.

She always cleaned the kitchen with a little help from Ellen but there was some queer game that the audience was playing with big balloons and hats and she just wasn't into it. So she kept flipping.

The doorbell buzzed.

Oh good, she thought. Now she had an excuse to put the damned hypnotic TV clicker down. She opened the door.

"Hey girl!"

"Wendy!" They hugged. "What the heck? I haven't seen you in months. Since Sammy's service. You're back in town. I love it."

"Yeah. Did I catch you at a bad time?"

"Nope. I was just cursing at Ellen."

"Cursing at Ellen? I didn't think anyone cursed at Ellen."

"I know. I'm weird." Audrey plopped on the couch. "Want a drink or something?"

"No, thanks." Wendy plopped next to her. I actually came to deliver this." She handed her an envelope. "Sammy left instructions with my Dad to give you and me one of these."

Audrey carefully opened the envelope. "He looooves his little notes huh?"

Wendy grinned.

"Oh, my God!" Audrey sat in shock staring at a check for $125,000. "I can't believe this."

"I know. I got one, too. Yours says the same thing in the comment line. The Singerman Fund. What does that mean, do you think?"

"Uhhh, that means that Sammy is pretty good at getting what he wants. That's what that means." Attached to the check was a piece of paper. "It's an application to LSU School of Engineering." Audrey looked up at the ceiling. "You're a tricky old bastard."

There was yet another envelope inside. It was folded in half and had the words "To Strippergirl: FOR YOUR EYES ONLY" printed on the outside. Destiny held it up to the light. "What's this?"

Wendy held her hands over her eyes. "Don't know. I just follow my instructions!"

"Hmmm. Okay then," Audrey said as she carefully tore open the envelope and pulled out the contents. There was a handwritten note inside that just read, "Did a little detective work using a drinking glass I stole from The Corner Bar – your friend, Ira."

Audrey opened the attachment, which was a printout of the lab results from a local laboratory in New Orleans. As she read on, tears welled up in her eyes. Her hands were shaking and she had to steady herself on the chair behind her. She sat down and read the words "Huntington's Disease Test Results: NEGATIVE."

She could barely catch her breath and she was vaguely aware of Wendy bending over her asking if she was all right. "Yes. Yes," she finally answered. "I'm fine. Oh, God. Yes. I'm really fine!"

"Good! You can tell me all about it in the car."

"Where? In the car?" Audrey asked.

"Yes. There's more." Wendy grabbed her by the hand and led her downstairs and out to a rental car. Behind the wheel was Barry and next to him was Walter. Audrey and Wendy hopped in the back seat. "Hi, Mr. Levine. Hey, Walter!"

They both smiled and waved.

"So what's up?"

Wendy reached down and lifted up an urn that was emerald green and emblazoned with "Sammy" in a typeface you'd see on a bowling ball. Audrey laughed hysterically.

Wendy handed her an official looking document that was titled THE SAMMY LEVINE BUCKET LIST. She read it aloud:

"The following are my LAST ADVENTURE wishes. I would like these to be completed by my son, Barry; my granddaughter Wendy; my trusted friend Walter Smith and my other granddaughter Audrey (who is probably still a stripper but not for long).

1. Visit LSU. I'd love to "see" it again. My reunion is coming up. While you're there visit the Admissions office and drop off Engineering Application. (Audrey smiled)

2. I'd love to go bowling again. If Walter is there, we can get free games. (Walter shook his head "no")

3. The guy who owns the Corner Bar jazz club where Holtzman's was on Frenchman Street told me that he would be happy to let Barry sit in for a few songs.

I would love to "hear" him play. (Barry gave a thumbs-up)

4. There's a Shooting Range in Metairie. I think it's a good place to get out frustrations. Wendy can put pictures of old bosses and boyfriends up. ("Yes!" Wendy said).

5. .You can dump my ashes at the Lakefront where Esther is. Always hated that place because of the snooty people who lived there ... but I want to rest next to Miss Esther."

Audrey grabbed the urn and squeezed it tight. Then she planted a big red lipstick kiss right next to Sammy's name. "Oh, you great big pain in the ass, ornery, asshole, wonderful man!!" They all smiled and patted the urn in Audrey's lap.

Audrey leaned in one last time and whispered to Sammy "I love you ... Grampy."

CPSIA information can be obtained
at www.ICGtesting.com
Printed in the USA
BVHW042329141118
533145BV00001B/2/P